"I swear, Kyle, sometimes you're so charming I think you must be part Southern."

"It's not charm. It's the truth." His hand tenderly captured hers, his thumb tantalizing her palm. "And for the record, Southern men don't have a monopoly on complimenting smart, beautiful, giving women."

Was it possible for bones to actually melt? Sure seemed like hers were. Even knowing it was a bad idea, Shayna couldn't seem to keep her hand from flipping over, her fingers tangling with his. "I think the wine might be going to our heads."

"I'm dead sober and dying to kiss you." His voice was so strong and deep, Shayna felt the words all the way down to her toes.

Dear Reader,

Welcome to Land's Cross! You've picked a wonderful time for a visit. Christmas means the Noël Festival: parades, parties and people donating their time to make the season brighter.

But this year, the holiday season also brings trouble for our friend Shayna Miller. Her birth father surfaces, offering her a million dollars to publicly endorse his version of their history. Problem is, his version isn't the truth. Worse yet, the truth could damage her "daddy's" reputation.

Personally, attorney Kyle Anderson doesn't agree with his client's plan, but until he makes partner, he doesn't have the luxury of walking away from this case. Unfortunately, he's underestimated Shayna's backbone— not to mention just how strong her convictions are!

I really enjoyed playing with the notion of what a person *wouldn't* do for a million dollars.

Here's hoping life blesses us all with convictions and memories we wouldn't trade for any price!

Wishing you laughter and love,

Dawn

MOONLIGHT
AND MISTLETOE

DAWN TEMPLE

SPECIAL EDITION®

Published by Silhouette Books
America's Publisher of Contemporary Romance

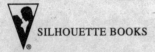

SILHOUETTE BOOKS

ISBN-13: 978-0-373-65492-5

MOONLIGHT AND MISTLETOE

Copyright © 2009 by Dawn Temple

Visit Silhouette Books at www.eHarlequin.com

Printed in U.S.A.

Books by Dawn Temple

Silhouette Special Edition

To Have and To Hold #1860
Moonlight and Mistletoe #2010

DAWN TEMPLE

was born in Louisiana and, despite having now lived more than half her life in Texas, in her heart, she still considers the Bayou State home. Everything about the South appeals to her: lazy days, nosy neighbors, old buildings and ancient trees. But the best thing is the people. In fact, her favorite part of writing is trying to honestly and emotionally capture that warm Southern spirit on the page. She loves to hear readers say they really connected with one of her characters— especially among the eclectic cast she uses to populate the background. Look closely. With any luck, you might recognize a few characters from your own life.

Dawn lives in the Texas Gulf Coast region with her husband, twin sons and three neurotic dogs. Stop by for a bit of Southern hospitality at www.dawntemple.com where friends are always welcome.

Writing a book is like raising a child, and this baby has been blessed by many mothers. Thanks and hugs go to:

—My own Thomas, Peake and Moore. You ladies helped conceive this story's bare bones, and I hope you'll be proud of how she's grown.

—Terri Richison, aka the Bionic Critiquer. You helped add life and love—not to mention blood, sweat and tears (literally). Friendship and support, above and beyond, on page and off. You rock!

—Susan Litman, my generous, patient and awesome editor. You provided the structure and guidance every awkward girl needs to grow into a beautiful woman. Thanks for never giving up on me or this story.

Chapter One

Shayna Miller gritted her teeth as she grabbed a handful of threadbare red wool and yanked at the hem of her borrowed Ms. Noel costume.

Good news—she managed to cover a bit more leg.

Bad news—her boobs nearly popped out.

Fearful any more tugging would shred the ancient fabric, she let the dress be and faced the mirror, frowning at the pregnant blonde reflected behind her. "This is going to be the first X-rated parade in the history of the Noel Festival."

"The dress isn't *that* tight." Lindy Monroe insisted. "Now, quit trying to change the subject. Tell me about Los Angeles."

Shayna had avoided her best friend—and this very conversation—since she returned to Land's Cross two days ago. Judging by the stubborn tilt of Lindy's chin, she wasn't going to let the matter drop until Shayna spilled the beans about the reunion with her birth mother, Patty Hoyt.

"It was horrible," she admitted sadly. "A huge waste of time and money."

"Her letter said she wanted to make amends." Lindy patted the bedspread near her hip. "So what went wrong?"

A resigned sigh shuddered through Shayna as she sat. The frightened little girl still huddled in her heart had naively hoped for a loving reunion, for answers to years' worth of unanswered questions. So much for childish wishes.

"Patty's still hustling the next big score. She only invited me to L.A. to talk me into helping with her current scheme."

"Which is…?" Lindy prompted.

"Seems my biological father is a big-shot psychologist who's been offered a ton of money to star in his own talk show."

"Wow. What's his name?"

"Steven Walker." Just saying his name made Shayna feel sick to her stomach.

"Ohhh. I've heard of him. He's done guest spots on nearly every daytime talk show."

"Yep. Turns out they had an affair while he was married, but he dropped her when she got pregnant with me. She said he paid her a bundle to keep quiet, but now she plans on scoring big."

"Why now?"

"She figures he'll pay anything to avoid tarnishing his reputation before the TV deal is officially signed."

"What a witch."

"That's not the worst of it." As it had when Patty first outlined her ridiculous plan, Shayna's anger began to spike. Her fingers trembled slightly as she unwound the band from her waist-length braid and began unknotting her hair.

"She wants me to go to some Who's Your Daddy clinic

and have a DNA test so she'll have hard evidence and can get even more money out of him."

Lindy laid a gentle hand on Shayna's knee. "Don't take this the wrong way, sweetie, but will people really care that he fathered a child out of wedlock twenty-five years ago?"

"I asked the same thing. Apparently, Dr. Walker's claim to fame, and the premise of his show, is family therapy, with an emphasis on old-fashioned, wholesome values. Ironic, huh?"

"Ouch." Lindy winced sympathetically.

Rehashing the encounter was making Shayna as antsy as a turkey in November. Her attempt to reconnect with her past had failed. All she wanted now was to keep moving forward.

Restless, she surged to her feet, but the costume's skirt remained bunched around her hips. Good Lord—the wavy mass of brown hair spilling over her shoulders covered more skin than this miserable dress! She skimmed her hands over her hips, but the snug material didn't budge.

"We've got to do something about this outfit before the festival starts."

Lindy, bless her understanding heart, ran with the defensive subject change this time. "Definitely. I can't believe old Mrs. Brinker ran it through the dryer. As petite as you are, I had hoped it might still fit."

"Petite?" Relieved to be discussing anything other than the soap opera Patty had wanted to make of her life, Shayna snickered. "That's just a fancy word for short as a stump." In her bare feet, she topped out at a whopping five-two. A very full-figured five-two.

"Imagine how that dress would fit if you were any taller."

"If I were any taller, it'd be little more than a belt, and the vice squad would raid the parade for sure."

"Nothing illegal about showing a little skin."

"A *little* skin? I look like a stripper from the North Pole."

"Yeah, but think about the fundraising possibilities. Thousands of dollars—singles, fives and twenties—tucked into your skimpy costume, one bill at a time. It would be the festival's most profitable year ever."

Lindy's ridiculous suggestion cracked Shayna up. Within seconds, they were both giggling like schoolgirls. The happy sound helped to chase away the cloud that had hung over her since her return from California.

For the first time since telling Patty to take a hike, Shayna began to relax. She'd always cherished her calm, uncomplicated life. For the past week, she'd worried her mother's vile drama would destroy her hard-won happiness, but that wasn't going to happen. She wouldn't allow it.

In the bedroom's far corner, the phone rang. Shayna skipped over to answer it, but one look at the caller ID brought her laughter to an abrupt halt. Over the past few days, the Southern California area code had become annoyingly familiar.

Lindy stopped giggling and sat forward quizzically. "Are you going to answer it?"

"No." Shayna's voice, and her answer, sounded weak.

Her recorded greeting filled the room, followed by a beep, then, "Ms. Miller. It's Kyle Anderson. *Again.*"

"Who?" Lindy mouthed, but Shayna waved her off as her one and only meeting with the man played in slo-mo across her memory's high-def, digitally clear screen.

She'd been standing in her hotel lobby, waiting on a cab to carry her to the airport, away from L.A. and her mother's world of make-believe. When he'd first stepped through the glass doors, his movie star good looks had her thinking she was on the cusp of a celebrity encounter.

Behind him, an elderly couple struggled to open the

door against the powerful Santa Ana winds. Before Shayna could react, Mr. Delicious hustled up, opened the door and ushered the thankful couple inside. His kind gesture and warm smile caused an unexpected stir of warm fuzzies in her belly. She'd always been a sucker for good manners.

Once the grateful couple moved off, he removed his sunglasses. As his gaze collided with hers, the warm fuzzies exploded into sizzling sparks. She stared openly, helpless to pull back from the most piercing blue eyes she'd ever seen. It was as though he looked straight into her soul. She'd felt simultaneously intrigued and challenged. Her pulse had skittered into high gear.

In a blink, his intense stare had been camouflaged behind a polished charm. A single dimple winked from his left cheek. He'd extended his hand and introduced himself in the same deep, powerful voice now pouring through her phone. Long distance didn't diminish the voice's effect one darn bit.

"It is urgent that I speak with you. A few minutes of your time, and we can put the whole matter to rest. Please contact me immediately."

He paused, then quickly rattled off his office and cell numbers. Shayna expected him to hang up. He always hung up after repeating his numbers. But the voice continued, his baritone plunging lower. "Ms. Miller, you can't keep running from me."

"Wow." Lindy enthused when the room was silent again. "Does he look as good as he sounds?"

"'Fraid so. Nearly six feet, broad shoulders, stunning blue eyes, sun-kissed blond hair. Your basic California pretty boy." Okay, that wasn't quite true. There was *nothing* basic about his looks.

"Sounds yummy. Who is he?"

"An attorney from Beverly Hills."

"Ooh la la. What's he want with you?"

"I'm not exactly sure. He said Dr. Walker hired him to 'contain the Patty Hoyt issue.'" Her fingers wiggled air quotes. "Then he started spouting some legalese about contracts and compensation, but I told him I had no part in Patty's plans, and I certainly wanted nothing to do with a hypocritical scumbag like his client."

"You didn't!"

"I did, but luckily my cab pulled up before I could say anything really nasty. I just told him to consider the *issue* contained and hightailed it out of there."

"Are you going to call him back?"

The answering machine's message-waiting light flashed red, like a danger signal. "No." She pressed the erase key. "I'm not interested in anything Dr. Walker or Kyle Anderson have to say. Too little, too late."

Despite the frustration boiling through his bloodstream, Kyle Anderson carefully returned the phone to its base. He had a hard-earned reputation as a cool cat here at Thomas, Peake and Moore, and he wouldn't dare let his guard down.

"Foolish girl." He chuckled for effect, knowing his boss, Roscoe Thomas, expected it. "She's playing hard to get."

"If she's avoiding your calls, why not pay her a visit like you did the mother? No one's better in person than you, Anderson. Especially with the ladies."

Kyle rolled his eyes. "The mother was easy."

"We already knew that. If she weren't, our client wouldn't be in this predicament."

He smiled again because it was expected. He sure as hell didn't see any humor in the situation. Years of hard work and sacrifice, and now his goal of becoming the firm's youngest partner hinged on the whims of a stubborn hick from Nowheresville, Tennessee? Not funny at all.

"I meant, Patty Hoyt was only after money. Her kind's easily dispensed with. Besides, the daughter has already left town, which makes me think she's got something bigger in mind."

"Like what?"

"This girl grew up dirt-poor while Walker's legitimate kids had every advantage money can buy. Judging by her bank records, she's still barely scraping by. Sounds like a recipe for revenge to me."

The glint of humor in Roscoe's eyes turned to steel. "Then stop her. Immediately." Still intimidating at sixty, Roscoe stood. "This is your chance, Anderson. Steven Walker pays a lot of salaries around here. He wants this matter resolved quickly, and the partners want him happy."

Kyle stood and crossed his arms. At a sniff under six feet, he had to cock his chin to meet Thomas's icy stare, but he dialed back the aggression with a cocky wink. "Leave Shayna Miller to me. Like you said, I'm good with the ladies."

"We can't afford to lose Walker." Thomas's voice turned as cold as prison bars. "You want a lucrative future with this firm, then do whatever it takes to get this girl on board before the press gets wind of any potential scandal."

Kyle kept his lips from snarling until after Thomas swaggered out of his office. He resented the ultimatum, but he didn't blame the old guy. Dangling the partnership as bait was a strong, strategic move, but damn, he hated occupying the weaker position.

He settled back into his high-backed leather chair and glared at the phone. After learning that Walker didn't intend to deliver the quick score she'd hoped for, Patty Hoyt had gladly provided Kyle with her daughter's number. He'd left Shayna Miller six messages since letting her slip away from the hotel. The annoying woman hadn't returned a single one.

The tiny doe-eyed girl he'd encountered in that hotel lobby couldn't have been further from what he'd been expecting. Unlike her overprocessed, overpainted mother, Shayna's skin had been naked and clear, a glossy peach lipstick her only ornamentation. She'd smelled like sunshine. After years of being assaulted by manufactured fragrances on women, the purity of her aroma had been intensely sensual. Most arresting, though, had been her wide, amber eyes. Clear, unguarded, welcoming.

All that had changed the instant he'd introduced himself and explained his connection to Steven Walker. She'd closed up. Her smile, her eyes, her attitude. Everything went blank, as if she'd flipped a switch and turned off her inner light.

He'd gone to that hotel for the very reason Thomas had just suggested. He'd intended to force the issue, do whatever it took to obtain her cooperation. But he'd failed. Not only had she fled before he could outline the lucrative details of Walker's offer but watching the wary distrust that replaced her initial shy smile had thrown him off his game.

Now, as he drummed a pen against his desk's blotter and plotted his battle plan, he once again cursed himself for squandering his opportunity to get a handle on Shayna Miller.

The longer he thought about that encounter, the more convinced he became that she'd been playing him. Complete lack of emotion was a learned skill, the kind of thing a calculating daughter would learn—or possibly inherit—from a calculating mother. The nut didn't often fall far from the tree.

So why the hell did his gut keep insisting he was misjudging her?

"It's just the voice," he assured himself as he flung the pen down and spread the Walker file out on his desk. That sexy southern accent had been playing on a continuous loop through his brain for nearly a week now.

Damned if he'd be swayed by slow vowels and exaggerated syllables. His future hinged on getting Shayna Miller to consent to the agreement Steven Walker was paying the firm megabucks to secure. And he didn't intend to fail.

He might not like his reputation as the office lady-killer, but he *had* been the one to negotiate Patty Hoyt's lump-sum payment—contingent upon her daughter's cooperation—in exchange for never bothering their client again. Ever.

So what if he despised this whole case? So what if he felt Walker's requests—both of the firm and the child he'd walked away from over two decades ago—skated ethical and moral lines. Personal feelings aside, his job was to satisfy the firm's most influential client, and until he made partner, that was all that mattered.

After he had his name on the letterhead, then he'd have the luxury of turning down clients who made his skin crawl, who reminded him of the human trash he'd grown up with. For now, he was one assignment away from achieving his professional goals and moving on to the next stage of his life plan: attractive trophy wife, two kids, a beach house in Malibu. By then, he hoped to hell his success would obliterate the image of the scrawny, unwanted street punk who still stared back at him in the mirror every morning.

An unusually frigid breeze swooped beneath the hem of Shayna's skirt as she scanned the crowd who'd turned out for today's ground breaking ceremony. Her teeth chattered as she snuggled deeper into her green-and-gold

Fighting Lions letterman sweater. Had she known winter planned to make a surprise appearance today, she'd have skipped the sweater's sentimentality and gone with her more practical—and much warmer—parka.

Numb fingers fluffed her hair out around her ears as she fought back sentimental tears. She loved this little tight-knit community. It was the day before Thanksgiving, with temperatures suspended in the mid-thirties, and still nearly a hundred folks were gathered in the town square to celebrate the official start of the James Miller Youth Center.

For nearly three years, she'd dedicated herself to making the youth center a reality, helping with everything from fundraising to building plans to investigating the best playground surface material. It was scheduled to open next spring, and she—and her newly completed social services degree—had already accepted the director's position. But to have the place named after her daddy? She couldn't imagine a greater honor.

He'd suffered a stroke and died seven years ago, so when the town council made the announcement earlier this year, she'd been too overjoyed to speak. They wanted to honor James Miller for his accomplishments with the high school football team—in the South, there was little that could top three consecutive state titles. But for her, his greatest accomplishment, the reason *she* celebrated his memory every day, was the fact that he'd saved her life. Blood relation or not, he was the only true parent she'd ever known. He'd stepped in when no one else wanted her and had chosen to love her and care for her and give her someone to love in return. He'd made them a family.

"How're you holding up, sweetie?" Lindy, who'd been smart enough to bundle up, sidled over to Shayna.

"Other than wishing I'd worn long pants, I'm fine."

"This weather is a shocker. Weatherman's calling for a thirty percent chance of snow for Thanksgiving."

"Judging by the wind blowing up my skirt, I believe him."

"What are you two pretty ladies whispering about over here?" Travis Monroe asked as he slipped an arm around his wife's expanding waist and pulled her snug to his side.

"Just griping about the weather," Lindy told him.

"Typical farm girls," Travis teased. He nodded toward Mayor Evans, who stood behind the podium as he got the ground breaking underway. "You ready for your big speech?"

"Yep," Shayna assured him. "I'm going to keep it short and sweet so we can all get back to our warm homes."

Just then, the mayor announced her name, and the crowd cheered and clapped enthusiastically. With a deep breath and a silent prayer, she took the podium. "I want to thank all of you for braving this unusual weather. Daddy would have been honored—and embarrassed—by this wonderful turnout."

Her voice began to wobble, forcing her to pause for a second, clear her throat, gather her composure. "James Miller was more than just a great coach. He was a great *man*. His calm, quiet demeanor hid an inner strength he gladly loaned to anyone who needed an extra push in life, and as you all know, he was uncomfortable with public kudos."

The sea of heads surrounding the podium nodded as one.

"I'll never forget the paper's headline after that first trip to state. 'Coach Miller Wins Title.' I was so proud, but Daddy said it wasn't true. He didn't win that title, the players did. So he rewrote that article, naming and praising the entire thirty-seven member squad. He wanted each of those boys to bask in the pride of their accomplishments."

A mumble rippled through the crowd, growing into

another burst of applause. Several teary faces stared back at her.

"That was typical. James Miller did great things every day and always preferred to shift the accolades to someone else. So today, in honor of his memory and because he's no longer here to deflect the praise—" she paused for a second as she accepted the gold-ribbon-embellished shovel the mayor handed her "—I proudly dedicate this site as the future home of the James Miller Youth Center, and I challenge us all to go out every day and do something great, just like he taught us to."

Sniffling back the tears she could no longer contain, she gingerly placed her high-heeled shoe over the shovel's edge and ceremoniously scooped out a bit of preloosened dirt. She lifted watery eyes, smiling and nodding at the crowd. Several loved and familiar faces smiled back, sending a wave of support and encouragement her way, helping her put a plug on her emotions.

Moving her gaze to the rear of the crowd, she spied an unanticipated and unwelcome spectator. Despite the icy nip in the air, a layer of cold sweat suddenly covered Shayna's skin.

Dark glasses protected his eyes, but his sun-bleached hair and blatantly expensive wool trench coat gave him away. The nerve of that man. What part of "not interested" did Kyle Anderson not understand?

With an effort, she pulled her attention back to the mayor as he offered his own words of praise. She listened with half an ear, her stomach pitching as Kyle wove his way through the crowd. She felt the pressure of his regard like a high-beamed spotlight and knew the locals wouldn't fail to notice a dashing, big-city stranger hanging around.

If asked—and in Land's Cross, being asked about your business was a sure bet—would he share his reasons for being in town? Would he blab about her unfortunate tie to Steven Walker?

Feigning calm, she smiled and clapped as Mayor Evans drew the celebration to a close. Shayna's inner wuss begged her to run as fast and far away as possible from the threat of Kyle's presence. But her pride shushed her fear, giving her the strength to march calmly and confidently in his direction.

Between them, the throng of well-wishers formed a gauntlet she had to kiss and hug her way through. By the time she stood face-to-face with Kyle, the community's love and support had steadied her backbone. Land's Cross was *her* turf. She had home field advantage. Let him take his best shot.

She accepted his outstretched hand, her smile so brittle she feared her cheeks would crack. "Kyle Anderson. What an unexpected surprise." She kept her voice as cordial as possible, hoping folks would assume he was as harmless as everyone else.

"This was too important for me not to come." He tugged her a few steps outside the crush before dropping her hand and leaning in to whisper, "Patty wanted to come, too, but I convinced her to give me one more chance before she traveled all this way."

Nausea boiled in her stomach at the mere idea of her bleach-blond bimbo mother invading Land's Cross— her home, her sanctuary. Anger surged through her system, demanding action, but pure stubbornness kept her from bolting. "That sounds an awful lot like blackmail, Mr. Anderson."

"I prefer to think of it as smart negotiating, Ms. Miller. I gave you the opportunity to set a convenient, *private* time and place to discuss matters, but you've forced my hand."

The fact that he had a valid point fueled Shayna's churning temper. Her stubborn refusal to return his calls had backfired. Big-time.

Hyperaware of the curious looks shooting their way, she shifted her body farther from Kyle's and nodded and waved at the nearest clutch of people.

"Mr. Anderson, I admit that not taking your calls was cowardly, and I give you my word that I will rectify the mistake. But only if you promise to keep Patty away from me and my home." She did her best to keep her face blank as she met Kyle's stare. Displaying her panic would sink her cause.

"Agreed." He pointed to Dixie's Diner across the street. "How about we get out of the cold and discuss Dr. Walker's proposal over a hot cup of coffee?"

"No. Not in public. We've given the gossips enough to chew on already. Besides, I'm busy right now." Maintaining a forcefully civil expression, she nodded goodbye and started to turn back to the crowd.

His hand snagged her wrist and stopped her escape. "Tomorrow then?"

"Tomorrow's Thanksgiving, and I'll be busy then, too. You'll have to wait till Friday." She tugged her arm free and took a step backward. The heel of her shoe caught on a clump of dirt, and she started to stumble.

Kyle reacted quickly, catching her around the waist and steadying her. Her chin grazed his broad chest. He smelled like fresh air and sun-warmed leather. For a split second, she entertained the fantasy of melting into him, of huddling into the heat that radiated from him, but his words instantly counteracted her body's momentary weakness.

"Don't abuse my generosity, Ms. Miller. If I have to track you down again, I won't be so understanding. Or subtle."

Alarmed by her own weakness as much as his audacity, she tipped her chin up and glared at him. "Turn me loose," she ordered briskly.

"If you insist." He relaxed his hold immediately, and she scurried back a step.

"Shayna? Everything okay over here?" Travis's voice sounded deeper and meaner than usual. Grateful for the interruption, she turned to find Lindy and Travis shooting visual bullets over her shoulder.

"You bet." She hoped her big, goofy grin would help sell the lie. "Mr. Anderson was just leaving."

"Anderson?" Lindy's brows rose. "From California?"

"Yes ma'am." Kyle flashed Lindy the same warm smile he'd shown the elderly couple back in Los Angeles, but here in Land's Cross it missed its mark. Lindy's expression didn't soften one bit.

Dropping the smile, he extended his hand to Travis and introduced himself. "Kyle Anderson."

Travis, a dyed-in-the-wool problem solver, accepted Kyle's hand, but his gaze remained pinned on Shayna. She knew he'd see her nerves plain as day and do what he could to set things right. But this was one problem she had to solve herself.

She spoke up quickly, before Travis could intervene. "Mr. Anderson, as I've explained, now is not a good time for me. Please call me later to discuss this matter."

"Certainly, Ms. Miller. I have your number." A flash of something Shayna chose to interpret as respect lit Kyle's sparkling blue eyes. "Until then."

Deliberately taunting her, he extended his hand for a goodbye shake. Refusing to be intimidated, she closed the gap and slipped her hand into his. Rather than immediately releasing it, he tugged her closer and lowered his voice.

"The clock is ticking, Shayna. We *will* talk." He leaned a smidge closer and added, "Soon."

His warm breath wafted against her cold ear. She couldn't contain the shudder that danced down her spine, but privately, she insisted it was just the weather.

As she watched, he climbed into a clean but wimpy gray rental car and drove off. Relief nearly buckled her knees.

"Oooh, you were so right about the pretty boy thing." Lindy's excited voice recaptured Shayna's attention.

"Shayna, who was that guy? Are you sure everything's okay?"

Touched by Travis's unwavering concern, she reached up and lovingly patted his cheek. "I'm fine, Papa Bear." For now, at least. "I'll explain everything tomorrow, okay? For now, I just want to go home and recharge." She gave them both a quick hug and a kiss then dashed to the safety of her sturdy old hatchback. She cranked the engine and waited for the heater to warm up.

Wishing for the hundredth time she'd never opened that stupid letter from her mother, Shayna forced her sticky transmission into gear and headed home. Mind spinning, she drove out of town and up the mountain to the cabin that had been in the Miller family for generations.

Kyle's dogged determination had her mind reeling. What in the world could Walker possibly want with her? He hadn't shown her one iota of interest in twenty-five years. He darned sure hadn't been interested all those nights Patty had passed out, leaving a very young Shayna essentially alone. And what about the times her mother had been arrested and Shayna had been shuffled into and around the overcrowded foster care system?

No, the only person who'd cared for her then had been James Miller, the kindhearted schoolteacher who'd lived next door. He'd cared enough to petition the courts for temporary custody. A single man with no biological or legal ties. Talk about an uphill battle.

And now, all these years later, Dr. Steven Walker pops up out of nowhere and sics his bulldog lawyer on her, egotistically expecting her to drop everything to accommodate his wishes?

Well, James Miller's daughter didn't kowtow to bullies. She'd honor her word and give Kyle Anderson thirty minutes to speak his piece; then she'd send him and his sleazy client packing.

Chapter Two

Shayna snapped her eyes open and stared at the cabin's vaulted ceiling, trying to figure out what had disturbed her nap. Snuffly snores drew her attention to the floor next to the couch, where her hundred-pound German shepherd snoozed. She rolled over and smiled at the sleeping giant—not much of a guard dog, but for her, Brinks was the perfect companion.

She registered the muffled crunch of tires on gravel half a second before the sound of a car door slamming finally roused the dog—and answered the what-woke-me-up question. Brinks jumped to his feet and ran to the front window.

She sat up just in time to see a masculine silhouette move across the curtain. Dread set her teeth on edge. She wasn't surprised that Kyle Anderson had tried to follow her home, but she was *flabbergasted* that the stubborn fool had succeeded. There were no street signs on the mountain.

Here, directions were given in terms of burned barns and tree stumps.

She was still several steps from the door when he knocked. Brinks rushed forward, a low growl sneaking past his bared teeth. Shayna laid a reassuring hand on his head. "Sorry, pup, but his spoiled city hide is probably too tough to chew."

Secretly wishing she were ornery enough to ignore him, Shayna pushed back the curtain. Other than his flapping coattails and wind-tossed hair, it was like someone had superglued an immovable statue to her front porch. A two-hundred-year-old oak should be so sturdy.

Over his shoulder, the sky sagged low and gray. While she'd napped, this morning's bad weather had turned downright nasty. If the temperature kept falling, there'd be sleet before nightfall. Which made getting rid of her uninvited guest even more critical.

Mentally gearing up for battle, she shooed Brinks out of the way and opened the door. A blast of frigid air whipped across the front porch, spilling a hunk of thick blond hair across Kyle's forehead before racing through the narrow wedge of the open door.

His gaze flicked over her, head to toe. She knew she looked sleep-rumpled and sloppy but darned if she'd fidget and primp for him. "Yes?" She didn't hold the door open or invite him in out of the cold. Rudeness went against her grain, but sometimes a girl had to break the rules.

His nose glowed Rudolph-red, yet he somehow managed to appear patiently inquisitive, as though he could wait all afternoon if need be. "You don't look too busy at the moment. Perhaps now's a better time for our discussion?"

Shayna bit her cheek to keep her lips from curving. Despite her pique over this man's nerve, she couldn't help but admire his tenacity. He'd have made one heck of a defensive tackle. Eye on the quarterback and don't stop running till you've mowed him down.

Only problem was, that made her the quarterback—but she planned to stay on her toes till the end of this game. Which meant she had to maintain control.

"Fine. But let's make it quick. The storm's moving in." She stepped back and reluctantly invited him in.

Kyle shuffled forward a step, and stopped immediately when Brinks issued a growled warning, his bared-tooth snout level with Kyle's most vulnerable parts.

She grabbed the dog's leather collar and attempted to pull him back, but the mutt refused to budge. "As you see, he's a mite overprotective, so you'd best mind your manners."

"Hey, boy." Kyle spoke softly, holding his palm near Brinks's snout. The dog took his time before accepting the offered sniff, and rather than his customary lick of approval, Brinks backed off just enough for Kyle to enter, then sat, keeping their visitor well within his sights.

Bolstered by the rare glimpse of Brinks's underused guard dog skills, Shayna pushed the door closed against the wind's pressure. She had promised to hear Kyle out. She hadn't said a thing about being pleasant.

"You've got fifteen minutes, Mr. Anderson. One cup of coffee and then you're gone."

Kyle's jaw ached with the effort of keeping his teeth from chattering. His custom-tailored suit and silk-lined Armani wool coat were no match for the frigid temperature and howling wind. He'd held on to his stern posture by willpower alone, but Christ, he'd been seconds from folding when she'd finally opened the door.

Of course, he'd prefer death by icing to having that

behemoth dog pin him to the wall by his balls. He wanted that partnership, but he didn't want it that badly.

Keeping one eye on Cujo, he assessed Shayna's personal space, looking for insight into her character, the kind of impressions and vibes you couldn't access through paper trails.

The cabin's spacious main room had the wide-open feel of a converted warehouse loft. In L.A., this space would rent for a small fortune. Wide-planked pine floors bore the scars and marks of old age beneath a sheen of polish. The furniture was an eclectic mix of new and old, littered with an abundance of odd-shaped pillows in every color imaginable. The overall effect was vivid and energetic, yet still homey and comfortable.

"Great space." He followed her to the kitchen, trying not to notice the sway of her full hips or the way her black leggings hugged her short but shapely legs.

"Thanks." She gestured toward a sturdy oak chair. "Sit."

The pony she called a dog was sprawled out in front of the fridge, his jet eyes sparkling, as if the mutt found humor in her ordering Kyle around. Refusing to be intimidated by a house pet—or his fierce-looking owner—Kyle removed his damp coat and threw it over the vacant chair she'd indicated.

"I'd prefer to stand." He leaned against the counter.

"Suit yourself." Neither of them spoke while she got the coffee going. When she turned, the glint in her sleepy amber eyes warned him she intended to fire the first shot.

"So, tell me, Mr. Anderson—" she folded her arms and glared at him "—what kind of proposal does Dr. Walker have for his bastard daughter?"

Her bluntness surprised him. He'd expected her to dodge the point as long as possible. "You're aware of Ms. Hoyt's plan to blackmail my client?"

"Yes, but I made it clear to her that I don't want any part of it."

"Unfortunately, she's decided to proceed anyway."

"I figured as much, but regardless, Patty's actions have nothing to do with me."

"That's a very naive statement, considering your mother's blackmail threats center around *your* birth."

She shrugged. "Perhaps, but without my help, her claims are just hearsay, right?"

"Hearsay?"

She spun and started rummaging in the cabinets but not before he saw the tinge of pink staining her cheeks. When she blushed, she reminded him of the first time he'd seen her. All that naturally unadulterated beauty in a sea of silicone implants and hair extensions.

"I'm a big *Law & Order* fan," she mumbled, pulling down a couple of coffee cups and filling them.

"Me, too." He accepted the cup she handed him, handle out, to avoid the possibility of brushing fingers. "Without your corroboration, her claims would indeed be hearsay, if the matter went to trial, but Patty isn't threatening to sue Dr. Walker in a court of law. She intends to drag him through the court of public opinion."

"Ah." She smirked, intelligence sparkling in her eyes. "A much more dangerous venue for your client, to be sure."

Kyle hid an unexpected grin behind his cup. He'd always admired women with quick wits. "In light of recent career developments, my client is justifiably interested in maintaining his good public reputation."

She snorted, obviously not buying his PR spiel. "Either way, I won't become involved. If your client wants to keep his ex-mistress quiet, why doesn't he just pay her off?"

"Because this isn't the first time she's promised to take the money and disappear forever."

She didn't look a bit surprised. "Still not my problem."

"True, but you are a part of the solution." Offering her his most reassuring smile, he removed a bulky envelope from his breast pocket. "Dr. Walker and I have formulated a simple resolution, one that insulates both himself and you from Patty's threats, both present and future." He held the envelope out. "Take a look. It's a very…generous compromise."

Kyle's wording was eerily similar to what he'd told her in that hotel lobby. Unsettled, Shayna took the envelope and slid a shaky forefinger under the seal. Instinct told her this would not be good.

Watching the papers emerge, she felt as anxious as a tourist at a snake-charming demonstration. Rationally, she knew the papers couldn't harm her, but that didn't stop her inner warning alarms from clanging ninety to nothing.

Her teeth worried the inside of her lower lip as the pages slipped free. Atop the bundle was a cashier's check, made out to her, for two hundred fifty thousand dollars.

Stunned, she tentatively touched the dollar amount, half expecting the check to be a mirage. When it didn't vanish under her fingers, she forced her slack jaw back into place. A familiar sick pain twisted in her gut. Patty had said Walker would pay big bucks to keep Shayna's existence a secret, and she'd been right.

So much for her hope that the other fifty percent of her DNA contained a smidge of human decency. Obviously, Patty Hoyt and Steven Walker were cut from the same cloth.

"Ms. Miller?" he asked gently.

Floundering to make sense out of what was happening, she shifted her focus to his face. One side of his mouth kicked up, cranking his dimple to life. That pleased, confident smile brought the entire bizarre situation into crystal clear focus.

This man expected her to be thrilled, to simply agree to whatever Walker had in mind, pocket the check and send him on his merry way. No doubt with a grateful hug and hearty thank-you. She'd never been so disappointed or outraged in her entire life.

"Shayna?" Kyle's normally robust voice was smoother than fresh cream. "I'm sure that much money comes as a shock—"

"Shock? It's an insult!" she hissed. She could practically feel the blood draining from her face. Brinks immediately scrambled to his feet and came to stand at her side, his massive body braced against her hip.

Her temper, which normally took forever to erupt, rose to a full boil as she bundled the wad of papers, check and all, and chucked them at the trash. They bounced off and landed under the table. The placid look on Kyle's face melted into confusion, but not even temporarily rendering him speechless could lessen Shayna's anger.

"What does your no-good client expect in return for a quarter of a million dollar payoff, Mr. Anderson? Maybe he wants me to murder Patty and bury her body on my mountain?"

"No, of course not. Shayna, calm down—"

"Calm down! I don't think so. How dare that…that—" she couldn't come up with a word vile enough to describe Dr. Walker "—that *man,* try to buy me off." The last words emerged as a shriek, but she was beyond caring. How dare he suggest she sell her pride.

Hands fisted at her sides, fury blackened the edges of her vision. "He's afraid of what Patty's information will do to his precious reputation, so he sends you down here with a counteroffer. Of all the rotten, lowdown, dirty—"

"Shayna!" Kyle's shout ended her tirade. She barely heard Brinks's growl over the roaring in her head. Kyle grabbed her arms and gave her several firm shakes. "Breathe, Shayna, breathe."

Shocked, she drew in a gulp of air. Her temper had never before gotten so out of hand that she nearly passed out. Hell, she didn't even know she could get that mad.

"Better?" Kyle asked gently, slowly releasing his hold on her arms.

Embarrassed, she nodded. Fearful her knees would give out any second, Shayna threaded her fingers into Brinks's fur and tensed every muscle in her body. "Your time is up, Mr. Anderson. I think you should leave now."

Brinks seconded the order with a teeth-baring snarl.

Barely holding herself together, she marched back to the front door, listening to the slap of Kyle's thin-soled shoes and the patter of Brinks's nails crossing the wood floor behind her. Her fingers shook as she yanked the door open. Another gust of wind roared inside, but she was too numb to feel the cold. Anger made an excellent insulator.

Kyle tossed a last wary look at Brinks. If not for the dog, Shayna knew Kyle wouldn't have left without a fight. Feeling deflated, she leaned against the door and waved Kyle toward the front porch. Unfortunately, he stopped in the open doorway and turned to face her. His unexpected maneuver put them much too close for rational verbal communication, but pure stubborn pride wouldn't allow her to back off a step.

He put a knuckle under her chin, leaving her no choice but to meet his gaze. Gone was his practiced charm and polish. All she saw was kindness and concern. The warm combination made her as light-headed as her earlier debilitating burst of temper.

"I'm sorry to have upset you, Shayna, but you have to realize this isn't over. Please read the agreement. You'll see that Walker's only trying to make things right."

He sounded so convincing that it took her a second to remember he was a master player, a lawyer, a professional manipulator. A man not to be trusted.

Frowning, she stepped back from his tempting touch and straightened her spine, doing her best to look strong and intimidating. "You can tell your client that unlike my mother, *I* cannot be bought." Then, before he could respond, she slammed the door in his face.

Kyle swore viciously as his dumpy rental slogged down the curvy mountain road. This should have been a one-day assignment. Get in, get her signature and get out. He hadn't expected to be delayed by a tiny package of grit and pride. Shayna Miller's disdainful glare had made him remember what he'd once been—the delinquent son of a two-bit criminal, a kid without hopes or dreams. A kid without a future.

But that kid was gone. Kyle had locked him away a long time ago.

The tires squealed as his foot agitated the accelerator. The car zoomed too fast around a corner, sending the tail end flying dangerously close to the mountain's edge and his briefcase to the passenger floorboard. He eased off the gas. Struggling to regain his composure, he drew in a lungful of dry, forcefully heated air.

Law had been an ironic yet deliberate choice. He'd vowed to become his father's complete opposite. He'd worked hard, graduated at the top of his class, and after taking a grunt position at Thomas, Peake and Moore, had worked his way up, establishing a reputation for unconventional yet effective tactics while always working within the bounds of the law. Seeing that stricken look on Shayna's face had made him feel like a heartless jackass, no better than the Walkers and Patty Hoyts of the world.

She obviously despised Patty and Walker, and he couldn't blame her. At least she'd lucked out and somehow landed with James Miller, who, from all reports, had managed to give her a mostly happy childhood. That put her miles ahead of most children in that situation.

Still, his instincts kept insisting something didn't add up. Most people would be overjoyed to receive a quarter of a mil, but not Shayna. She had freaked out, gotten so overwrought she nearly passed out.

Although, he had to admit that the melodramatic line about murdering Patty had almost been funny—until her face had turned blue. She'd reminded him of one of his foster sisters, who used to hold her breath until whatever adult was in charge gave in to her demands.

Was that it? Had she—like her mother—put on an act and tried to play him for a fool? Her response had been frighteningly real, but a good con woman needed Oscar-caliber acting skills.

The ping of his BlackBerry cut off his internal line of questioning. He was expecting word regarding pieces of Shayna's background report that hadn't been completed this morning when he'd left L.A. Maybe whatever information Amanda, his secretary, had dug up would explain whether Shayna's irate, over-the-top response to Walker's offer was genuine or not.

Amazed to be getting cell reception amid the massive, shadowy trees and steep, rounded slopes, Kyle made a grab for his fallen briefcase and the cell phone tucked inside. The lightweight car veered to the right. Jerking upright, he overcorrected. The tires skied over the road's glassy surface, sending the car sideways down the mountain. The tail flared, throwing him into a full skid.

Hands gripped tightly at ten and two, Kyle steered into the skid. The drum of adrenaline rushing through his brain blanketed out all sounds. His lungs froze. Suddenly the swirling stopped, replaced by a swift loss of altitude. The car hit ground with enough force to rattle his skull but not enough to deploy the airbags.

Inertia slammed him against the doorframe. Cautiously he flexed his muscles. His head felt ready to split open, and his knees, which had jammed into the steering column, stung like a son of a bitch.

He rolled his neck to check the view out his window. A relieved breath shuddered through him. The landscape tilted at a forty-five-degree angle, the car's grille was buried nose down in the ditch, but he hadn't gone over the edge.

Hands shaking, he shoved the door open with his shoulder and crawled out of the crumpled car. Wind and freezing rain slapped his face. He ducked back in, retrieved his coat and shrugged it on before snagging his briefcase off the passenger floorboard.

He scrambled up the steep embankment as fast as he could, slipping to his knees several times in the icy mud. Night was falling quickly, the already-freezing temperature plummeting, the rain lashing at him furiously.

Once he reached the road, he took shelter under a large tree. It blocked the deluge, but the wind continued to roar under the canopy of branches. To his right, something rustled through the underbrush just as the sun disappeared. Nature towered above him, blocking the moonlight, but the crooked beam of his headlights bouncing off the side of the ditch showed Kyle all he needed to see.

She was to blame for this mess.

She had him so frustrated and confused that he'd gotten careless.

She, with her sexy Southern drawl, her stubborn refusal, her well-portrayed outrage.

And whether she knew it or not, Shayna Miller had escalated the stakes. Now it was more than just business.

Now it was personal.

Shayna took Kyle's advice and read Dr. Walker's "generous" compromise. Definitely a shocker. By all rights, she should be even more livid than when she'd seen the check. No one would blame her if she suddenly burst into tears or started flinging breakables against the wall, but at the moment all she felt was numb. Overwhelmed. Lost.

Tossing the offending document onto the coffee table, she pushed to her feet and stood in front of the fireplace. Stirring up the flames helped melt away a layer of disbelief. As did imagining feeding the annoying papers to the hungry fire.

When she'd first seen that check, she'd been terrified. What would a man like Walker demand in exchange for such an obscene amount of money? Turned out the quarter mil was only a down payment. The full agreement, which turned out to be little more than an appalling, drawn-out employment contract, promised her a million dollars if she cooperated.

Wanted: one formerly mistreated and unwanted child to play the part of Dr. Steven Walker's long-lost, much-loved and stupidly forgiving daughter. Experience as Patty Hoyt's stooge preferable. Ethics: optional. Pay: one million dollars. Office hours: one hour on live television—as the surprise guest for the debut episode of Dr. Walker's new talk show.

She could practically see the tagline: Benevolent father and prominent family therapist welcomes daughter he never knew into his happy family, saving her from a lonely life of poverty and despair.

What a load of malarkey. Or was it? All Shayna had to go on was Patty's word that Walker had paid her off when he'd learned she was pregnant. Hell, even that much of her backstory could be a lie.

Sagging against the arm of the couch, she rested her sock-covered feet on the hearth. Walker's offer did come with one very appealing caveat. In return for Shayna's cooperation, he would pay Patty fifty grand a year for life, providing mommy dearest didn't so much as blink in Shayna's direction.

That kind of peace held way more appeal than a million-dollar bribe. Not that any prize could ever tempt her to agree to such a ludicrous plan.

She couldn't believe that pompous jerk actually thought she'd go on national television and tell the world her daddy hadn't taken good care of her. Sure, money had been tight in the Miller household, but they'd always had everything they needed. She'd had a far better life than a lot of kids. A hell of a lot better than the life she'd been living before James Miller became her daddy.

Letting her body fall backward, Shayna lay across the couch, staring up at the portrait over the mantel. It had been taken at the annual Moonlight and Mistletoe Ball. She'd been ten, with Bugs Bunny teeth and her first pair of high-heeled shoes. Daddy had looked handsome despite the four-inch-wide red-and-gold tie she'd insisted he wear, because it matched her new dress.

Even now she still considered it one of the happiest nights of her life. Despite the complete lack of physical similarities, the picture screamed family.

And now Kyle Anderson, her personal messenger of doom, had delivered a bizarre request that threatened everything she'd ever cherished. Dredging up her and James Miller's past on national television would stir up entirely too many questions. With answers that could very well mean the end of her life as Shayna Miller.

Chapter Three

Kyle had managed to talk himself out of his unjustified anger with Shayna during the forty-minute hike back up the slick, icy mountain. He'd decided to withhold judgment on whether or not she was playing him until he'd had a second chance to thoroughly outline Walker's plan. But after standing in the freezing rain, banging on her blasted door for five minutes, his good intentions had vanished. His fury rocketed back to full force.

She had to be in there. The damned weather had them both trapped on this mountain. No way he was going to freeze to death while she sat in her toasty cabin and ignored him.

The door finally swung open. Warm air brushed against his face but didn't do a damn thing to thaw his temper. "What the hell took you so long? It's damn cold out here!"

"Ex-*cuse* me?" Shayna tossed a mass of wet hair over her shoulder.

The apology he knew he owed her froze in his throat. Damn, but she was beautiful. Freshly showered, smelling like vanilla, her sensuous hair hanging loose to her waist, her curvy body wrapped in the most atrocious robe he'd ever seen.

Desire scorched through him. He barged inside, no longer aware of the cold that seconds before had nearly turned him into a block of ice. His briefcase slid from his grip and landed on the floor, unheeded by them both. Standing this close, her intoxicating aroma made him light-headed. He swayed forward, his hands intent on touching her skin, but his aim was thwarted when she rushed him, grasping his biceps, her face scrunched in concern.

"Kyle?" The urgency in her voice cracked through the fog in his brain. "Are you all right?"

Hell no, he wasn't all right.

Pulling himself together, he stepped away. As soon as he'd cleared the way, she shut the door behind him. Without the benefit of the mountain's wide-open spaces, the lamp-lit cabin felt too small, too intimate.

The concern in her amber eyes intensified. Again, she moved closer, this time with her hands aimed for his face. "You're bleeding."

At the touch of her warm fingertips against his freezing forehead, his icy blood melted, ratcheting his temperature to a dangerous degree. What the hell was wrong with him? The blow to his head must have knocked all his brain cells below his belt.

Desperate to restore his equilibrium, he swatted her hand away. Hurt washed over her expression, but of course, stubborn woman, she didn't back down. Instead, she snagged a box of tissues off the entry table and, after gesturing at his forehead, shoved them against his chest. "Care to tell me what happened?"

The terrifying experience replayed in his memory, re-igniting his earlier fear and anger. "You nearly got me killed, that's what."

Her face paled. "Killed?"

"Yeah." He flung out his right arm, gesturing toward the closed door. "You threw me out in a damned ice storm, and my car almost skidded off this godforsaken mountain."

Kyle had forgotten about Shayna's giant dog until the beast charged him, his enormous front paws pinning Kyle's shoulders to the door. Keeping one eye glued to the dog's bared teeth, he glanced at Shayna. The color had returned to her face with a vengeance.

To his surprise, she ignored her dog's threatening behavior. "First of all—" she ticked her point off with her index finger, as if preparing to recite a long list of his sins "—I didn't throw you out into anything. You showed up uninvited. Not my fault you chose to tackle the mountain in bad weather. Secondly," she said with another ticked finger, "you can hardly blame me if you aren't smart enough to slow down and take care on a dark, rainy night."

Her logical response angered him further. He hated stupid mistakes. Especially his own. "Who expects ice in November?"

The dog took exception to the vehemence in Kyle's voice. Brinks's weight pressed against him even more forcefully. Fist-sized paws branded his chest, restricting his airflow and threatening permanent damage to his ego.

"Think you can call your dog off?" he asked through gritted teeth.

"Not until we get a few things straight." She planted her hands on her hips, drawing the butt-ugly robe even tighter against her lush figure. "Obviously, if you drove your car into a ditch—"

He opened his mouth to object, but reminding himself of the power of silence decided to keep his thoughts to himself.

"—you're going to need a dry, warm place to sleep tonight. Unfortunately, Brinks and I don't offer shelter to rude jerks."

Cautiously, he raised both hands to his sides in modified surrender. "Please forgive me. I was angry with myself for being careless. I shouldn't have taken my temper out on you." Swallowing hard, he mustered up a charming smile. "Since I find myself at your mercy this evening, I hope I can convince you—and Brinks—to reconsider."

She nodded imperially, but the movement wasn't quick enough to hide the smirk flirting with the corners of her mouth. Seemed the price of her sofa was a slice of his pride.

She snagged Brinks's collar and wrestled the dog off his chest. Her robe slipped, exposing one creamy, delectable shoulder. He forced his eyes level with hers and ordered them to stay put as he remained pressed to the door, awaiting her verdict.

The dog, his watchful eyes glued to Kyle, backed up and sat at attention next to Shayna.

"Brinks and I have decided to accept your apology. You are welcome to the spare bed."

"Thank you." He moved away from the door, and his soaked shoes squished. How could he have forgotten how cold and wet his clothes had gotten while he'd traipsed around in the icy rain? "Can I also borrow your shower? And some dry clothes?"

"The shower, yes, but—" she eyed him from head to toe, her perusal warming him from the inside out "—I'm not sure I've got anything that'll fit you."

The middle-of-the-night huskiness in her voice hit him below the belt. He turned away, one hand propped on the paneled wall as he toed out of his drenched shoes. In his periphery, he saw her nibbling her bottom lip, toying with the length of hair draping over her generous breast, wordlessly assessing him. His discomfort—and suspicions—grew.

Were her nerves—like her earlier meltdown—legitimate or calculated? Were the ill-fitting robe and husky voice deliberate ploys designed to distract him? He could easily imagine Patty using sex to get her way, but Shayna? Sure, he'd seen her short fuse, but he'd also seen her fierce pride. She didn't strike him as the type to degrade herself that way, but desperate people often took desperate chances.

How far was Shayna willing to go to protect her secrets?

Testing her, he closed the distance between them. The color in her cheeks heightened, and the fingers twining through her hair trembled. He couldn't help but imagine the erotic tickle of those long strands sliding across his thighs.

She sidestepped him and let the dog outside. When she turned back around, her robe slid even more. He realized the exact instant Shayna's nervous fingers encountered the exposed skin of her shoulder. The red in her face deepened from embarrassed to horrified.

"Oh, my!" She clutched the warped collar in both hands as she started backpedaling toward the stairs. "Please excuse me for a moment. I need to, uh—" the hem of her robe flared as she swiveled and ran "—change."

At the base of the stairs, she stuttered to a slow stop. One hand released its death grip on her robe and grabbed the newel post so hard her knuckles turned white. She drew in several long, deep breaths before pivoting towards the room.

Her cheeks remained flushed, but her precise posture gave the impression of confidence.

"The bathroom's through there." She pointed to a door below the stairs. "It's connected to the spare room." Tension clenched her jaw, and her eyes didn't quite meet his, yet her voice betrayed none of her distress. "I'll see about finding you something to wear."

She didn't make it past the third riser before she stopped again. Kyle was pretty sure he caught the sound of a whispered four-letter word. With a heavy sigh, she turned and headed back down the stairs.

"I don't get many overnight guests, so I need to double-check and make sure there are clean towels in the bathroom." She crossed the den, both hands clutching at her neckline.

While he waited, Kyle laid his ruined shoes out in front of the toasty fire, hoping to hell they dried before morning. He shed his heavy, wet wool coat, looking around for something to prop it on. He stopped his scan when he noticed Walker's agreement on the coffee table. Dropping the coat next to his shoes, he picked up the papers just as Shayna reentered the room.

"Bathroom's all set, but I'm afraid you'll have to let the shower run for several minutes before you get any hot—" Her words and her feet came to an abrupt halt when she saw what he held. Her robe was very tidy and very securely belted.

"So." He saluted her with the papers. "You read it?"

The layers of composure seemed to visibly flake off her frame. "Yes." Slowly, she continued across the room.

"What do you think?"

"I think I should have made my terms clearer up front, Mr. Anderson." She took the papers and shoved them in her pocket. "Tonight's offer of hospitality is contingent upon your not speaking about anything or anyone mentioned in that agreement."

She'd ducked his question, but her formal wording provided all the confirmation he needed. "So what do you propose? We spend the evening staring at each other?"

"Of course not. Surely you can discuss matters outside your job. Current events? Movies? Coke versus Pepsi?"

Was she nuts? She expected them to engage in chitchat? The gash on his head throbbed painfully. He clenched his eyes and rubbed his fingers over his knotted forehead.

"Goodness, look at that scowl. A body'd think I suggested we spend the evening learning to macramé!" The musical vibrations of her laughter compelled him to reopen his eyes. All her earlier tension was gone. Her confidence and grace had returned. "Go ahead and start your shower. I'll see what I can dig up for you to wear and leave it on the bed. Then I'll scrounge up something for dinner."

Kyle couldn't help admiring the view as she disappeared up the stairs, her hair glistening like a stream of sable running down the center of her back, ending just above her swaying derriere.

So she had a healthy sense of humor to go with her temper. Kyle felt the corner of his mouth turn up at the image of the two of them, snuggled together on the couch, roaring fire and soft music in the background, mugs of steaming hot chocolate in their hands.

In his mind's eye, the cocoa—and that ugly green robe—suddenly vanished. The room's temperature skyrocketed as he imagined her nimble fingers undoing his belt.

A loud, ferocious bark from the front porch vanquished his fantasy vision. Good thing Brinks had such excellent timing. After a quick zipper check, Kyle let the dog inside. The beast gave him one indifferent sniff before racing into the kitchen.

He started unknotting his tie and headed for the

bathroom, thinking he might have to start with a cold shower. Tempting as it was to lose himself in the possibilities of being alone in a cozy, isolated cabin with an intriguing, sexy woman, he couldn't forget what was at stake.

His job.

His future.

She may have attempted to set out guidelines for their forced confinement, but no way in hell was he going to waste this prime opportunity. They were stuck with each other tonight, and like it or not, Shayna Miller would be discussing her father's proposal.

Who knew a big-city lawyer would be so discombobulated by the idea of strictly social conversation? The horrified look on Kyle's face had been priceless. Chuckling at the memory, Shayna pulled on a crew-necked, long-sleeved T-shirt and smoothed it over her hips. Good to know her sense of humor had survived the day from hell. She'd need it to endure the hours ahead.

While she'd showered, she sorted through all the surprises lobbed at her today, and she'd been forced to admit—to herself, at least—that Kyle wasn't to blame for the bombshell he'd dropped. He'd only been doing his job, and regardless how unsavory the message, he didn't deserve the full force of her anger.

That belonged to Walker and Patty.

Besides, what could a man like Kyle Anderson know about trying to put distance between yourself and your sleazy parents? More than likely, he'd grown up in a perfect Beaver Cleaver household where fighting over the television remote was the full extent of family strife.

A final check in the mirror assured her she was decently covered. Banishing all thoughts of Kyle Anderson and his ideal childhood, she grabbed her robe off the foot of the bed. The poor thing had seen better days and was stretched out nine ways to Sunday, but it had been a gift from Daddy and she treasured it. Funny how a ratty old scrap of material could feel like a warm hug.

If only seeing Kyle hadn't driven all rational thought from her head, maybe she'd have had the wherewithal to change clothes immediately instead of running around flashing him.

When she'd opened the door, he'd been fierce, primal and sexy as all get out. Her girlie parts had instantly flared to life. Heck of a time for her libido to raise its hand and demand attention.

Of course, Kyle had opened his mouth and spoiled the effect. It was going to be darn hard to treat him like an innocent messenger if his every word got her dander up.

She hooked the robe on the back of her bathroom door. Beneath her feet came the familiar vibration of well water rushing through the cabin's ancient copper pipes. Forcefully blocking out all thoughts of Kyle in her shower, Shayna straightened her spine and headed for her closet. She had to find him something to wear.

The first thing she thought of that had half a chance of covering his broad shoulders—which she *wasn't* picturing in her mind—was Daddy's old coaching gear. The fit would be questionable, but it beat the heck out of having Kyle running around in a towel until his things dried. Thinking pure thoughts, Shayna snagged the green-and-gold track suit—the only clothes she'd saved all these years—from the darkest regions of her closet.

Out of habit, she brought it to her nose. His scent had faded from the material but not from her memory. Old Spice, leather and pipe tobacco. Eyes misty, she returned the hanger to the back of her closet.

No way she could handle seeing Kyle Anderson wearing her daddy's coaching gear. That outfit represented the essence of James Miller. To allow Steven Walker's legal minion to borrow it—even if the alternative was a near-naked man in her house—felt like a betrayal.

Digging deep in the other corner of her closet, she unearthed a paint-stained sweatshirt, one she'd appropriated from a college boyfriend. She aimed herself at the mirror and held the sweatshirt up to her chest. Since she couldn't see herself around the gigantic black wall of material, she figured it would work. Now she just needed something to cover his bottom half. Out of the blue, memory struck. Shayna balled up the sweatshirt, quickly retrieved a thick pair of hiking socks and raced downstairs. A few months back, Travis had left a pair of coveralls here when he'd volunteered to fix her leaking dishwasher.

As she hit the first-floor landing, she paused for a beat, listening for the familiar rumble of the shower. Assured Kyle was still occupied—and no longer bothering to pretend she wasn't picturing him in her mind—she raced into the smaller of the two bedrooms, which had been hers as a girl.

On the other side of the wall, the shower sounds stopped. With a squeaky groan, Shayna kicked it into high gear. She *so* didn't want to be here when Kyle wandered out of the bathroom, most likely naked as a jaybird. The sweatshirt and socks landed on the bed as she rushed to the dresser. She pulled open the top drawer and dug through it. No coveralls. Same story for the second drawer. And the third.

Drat! They had to be in here somewhere.

She yanked open the bottom drawer, and just as her fingers connected with the folded piece of denim she'd been searching for, she heard the bathroom door open behind her.

Easily picturing him crossing the room buck naked, she jerked to her feet. "Don't come out yet," she ordered, blindly tossing the coveralls to the bed. "I was just leaving."

"No problem. I'm decently covered."

Not certain what a Hollywood pretty boy considered decent, Shayna turned slowly and had to bite her tongue to keep from sighing. Her stomach literally cramped at the delicious sight of him.

He had an oversized bath towel wrapped around his tight, flat waist. Holy cow, he had a great body. Who knew attorneys had six packs? And those shoulders? Wow! The entire beautiful package was coated in a golden California glow. Imagine. A tan in November.

Afraid she'd start foaming at the mouth if she allowed her inspection to wander any farther south, Shayna racked her brain for a sophisticated, blasé remark. Nothing there. Seemed she didn't have a single G-rated comment left in her head.

Surprisingly, Kyle bailed her out. He picked up the coveralls and held them to his chest. "The mechanic look isn't exactly my style, but beggars can't be choosers. Hell, I was afraid you'd make me wear that awful robe, and I'm sure I wouldn't have done it justice."

He threw her a wink before picking up the bundle of clothes she'd brought downstairs and returning to the bathroom. Completely stunned, Shayna sank onto the bed. She had to use her palm to close her gaping mouth.

So in addition to being stubborn, rude and doggedly determined to do Steven Walker's bidding, Kyle Anderson was also charming, funny and extremely hot. Talk about a lethal combination.

And since she was stuck with him for a while, she'd best find a way to put the man and the situation into perspective.

Pushing to her feet, she left the room, making sure to pull the door closed. Headed for the kitchen, she decided to deal with this the way she did most forms of stress. Food.

Since she wasn't alone, she'd have to forego her favorite comfort food—strawberry ice cream, straight from the carton. A nice everything-but-the-kitchen-sink sandwich sounded like a good second choice.

Then, hopefully, they could kill a couple hours before bedtime with a nice, safe family movie, or better yet, a sappy holiday special. Anything to keep her from dwelling on her heart-pounding reaction to Kyle Anderson.

The sound of him clearing his throat alerted her to his arrival. She looked up and had to fight to keep her eyes from rolling into her head.

Not fair. The man looked nearly as scrumptious in the baggy hand-me-downs as he did in the snug towel.

This was going to be an extremely long night.

Chapter Four

Kyle hadn't missed the spark in Shayna's eyes. Good to know the attraction wasn't one-sided. Although why the hell this ridiculous outfit turned her on was anyone's guess. The coveralls fit well enough through the shoulders, but they were too long in the leg. He'd been forced to cuff the pants to keep from tripping.

He'd left the enormous black hoodie on the bed, after a quick fantasy of Shayna parading around in it, her naked legs peeking out from a thigh-high hem.

The image had stirred him to half-mast. Now, seeing her standing barefoot in the kitchen, his desire swelled again. He raked a frustrated hand through his damp hair.

"Oh! You need to put some ice on that bump." As Shayna grabbed a plastic bag and turned to the freezer, he ran his fingers over the tender, swollen skin on his forehead. His X-rated fantasies had completely numbed the pain, but now that she reminded him, he did have a throbbing headache.

She wrapped the ice pack in a wet cloth and motioned him to the table. "Sit down and hold this in place."

He did as told, laying his damp clothes on the kitchen counter as he passed. The minute his butt connected with the well-worn wooden seat, she gingerly placed the cold press against his forehead then grabbed his hand and used it to hold the cloth in place.

"Ouch. That stings."

"Don't be such a baby. Just grit your teeth and do it. Otherwise, you'll have a huge goose egg by morning." She gently jabbed his shoulder before turning around and grabbing his laundry bundle. "Sit there while I get the washer started, then I'll dig up some aspirin."

Kyle turned in his chair, watching the enticing sway of her hips as she strolled down the narrow kitchen and into the attached mudroom. Despite the lingering pain from the crash, he felt pretty good. With a contented exhale, he rested his head against the back of the chair.

Shayna's obvious concern for his well-being did more for his aches and pains than a bottle of pain reliever ever could. No one had ever reacted that quickly to ease his suffering. It was the kind of luxury he hadn't planned for in his life but one he could definitely become accustomed to.

Only problem was, he couldn't imagine his future trophy wife even knowing where the kitchen was, much less risking her fifty-dollar manicure to make him an ice pack.

The edges of his contentment frayed. The closer he got to achieving the goals he'd set fifteen years ago, the more he questioned them. He'd based his life's accomplishments on an angry teenager's view of success. Wealth and power had been his primary motivators, but the messed-up kid he'd been had no idea what that kind of accumulation required.

But he was too close to the finish line to quit now. Dismissing his self-doubts, he concentrated on the homey sounds of Shayna bustling around the kitchen.

He'd never met anyone like her. She had made it emphatically clear she didn't want him here—not in Land's Cross and most certainly not in her home. Yet somehow, she'd managed to put that aside and treat him with kindness and respect.

The woman was almost too good to be true, and being an old-school cynic, Kyle found it difficult to take her at face value. No matter how tempting the offer.

The clunk of glass hitting the tabletop snapped his head upright. He dropped the ice pack and opened his eyes. Shayna stood mere inches from him, her vanilla scent tantalizing him, a pill bottle in her hand.

"Here, take a couple of these."

Their fingers touched as he accepted the bottle. A physical spark zinged up his arm. He knew she felt it, too, by the way she rubbed her fingertips together, as if trying to hold on to the sensation.

Kyle put the ice pack on the table and sat up, the pill bottle rattling with the movement. She stood so close that it would take very little effort for him to pull her onto his lap where he could feast on her generous mouth.

The tip of her tongue snuck out and wet her lips. Kyle's coveralls became skin tight. He started to reach for her just as her eyes widened. Nervous fingers twining through her hair, she backed away, not stopping until her backside hit the counter. With her gaze glued over his shoulder, she gestured behind her.

"Hungry?" Her raspy voice stretched the second syllable, drawing his body even tighter.

Hell, yes. Starving. And only one thing in that kitchen would satisfy him. Unfortunately, even if Shayna put herself on the menu, he'd be forced to abstain.

He'd come in here determined to charm his way under her defenses. A casual dinner, harmless small talk, whatever it took to get her to lower her guard. Yet less than ten minutes in and he'd let hormones distract him.

"Hope you like sandwiches." Her forcefully upbeat tone made it clear she wanted to pretend the past few minutes hadn't happened. He was more than willing to oblige.

He stood and, leaving as much distance between them as the cramped quarters allowed, approached the ingredients she'd laid out. Two kinds of bread, three varieties of lunch meat, precut slices of pepper jack cheese, a platter of fresh veggies, half a dozen jars of condiments and a giant bag of potato chips.

"It looks like a gourmet sandwich shop in here."

"Sandwiches are the closest thing to gourmet we get around here. Cooking's not my strong suit."

Hello, opening! He tried not to smirk, but man, she'd just lobbed a big, fat conversational softball right over the heart of the plate. Playing it cool, he casually leaned one hip against the counter. "Then what is your strong suit?"

An uneasy look flickered across her face. She fidgeted, as if she wanted to put more distance between them, but she held her position. He liked that about her. She didn't back down.

"Well, I'm good with people. Animals love me. And I'm a crack shot."

That last comment was a bit unnerving, but Kyle refused to back off. "All very fine recommendations, but what's the one thing you do better than anything else?"

"That's an intriguing question." She drummed her fingers against her chin, her eyes studying the kitchen's ceiling. "Oh! I've got it." She snapped her fingers. Her relaxed, friendly grin returned, stretching ear to ear. "I'm fantastic at making kids smile."

"How is that a skill?"

"Children often pay the highest price for their parents' mistakes. They can lose their trust in grown-ups. By winning back a little of that trust and making them smile, I can restore some normalcy to their chaotic lives. That's why I studied social services, so I can help kids who were dealt a raw deal in the parental lottery."

Ah, now this was something he could work with. "Not a very lucrative career choice."

"I'm sure I can scrape by. Besides, money's not as important to me as doing something worthwhile with my life."

"All the more reason for you to have a long-range savings plan. A million dollars would make a cozy nest egg."

Her quick wit showed in the simple, cocky way she arched her eyebrows. "Careful there, counselor. I'd hate for you to break the ground rules and end up sleeping outside."

Knowing when to push and when to back off, he waved his hands in mock protest before gathering up the cheese and lunch meat. "I'm just making conversation."

"More like *working* the conversation."

He shrugged. "Force of habit."

"I'd call it compulsive behavior." She grabbed the platter of veggies and followed him to the table. "So, how about you? What's your strong suit?"

Getting gals like you to cooperate with my clients' wishes.

Knowing that much honesty wouldn't win him any brownie points, he returned to the counter and gathered up the remaining sandwich makings before giving a less specific answer. "Talking people into seeing things my way."

"Guess that's why you decided to become a lawyer, huh?"

"Actually, I didn't really hone my communication skills until after college."

"So then why *did* you pick law?"

"I wanted to make a lot of money."

"Really? I kind of figured you grew up with money."

"Hardly." He snorted. Her brows crinkled, but he damned sure didn't want her to continue on that track, so he quickly followed with, "Lower middle class. Money never went far enough."

It was a true statement but not exactly an honest answer to her unasked question.

"So, if your goal was to be rich, why not become a doctor or an accountant or an investment banker or a rock star or any of a hundred other jobs that don't have such a negative reputation? Why law?"

He had to give the lady points for intelligence. And perseverance. She'd seen right through his flimsy excuse, and he was sure she'd peck at him till she found the truth. She'd have made a great attorney.

Might as well reward her with a slice of the truth.

"As a kid, I was a bit of a runt and always seemed to get the short end of the stick, so I decided early on that I wanted to be powerful and influential enough to ensure I always came out on top."

"And do you?"

"Most of the time."

"Huh." That single grunted syllable sounded very confused, and he expected more questions. Instead, she began building herself a massive sandwich.

He followed suit, all the while conscious of her mind still silently working its way through something. He knew her curiosity wasn't yet satisfied. What he didn't know was whether she would pursue more answers.

Halfway through the meal, she put her sandwich down and turned cautious eyes on him.

"Can I ask you a personal question?"

More personal than the ones she'd already asked? Hell, that could be dangerous. "You can ask, but I can't promise to answer."

She pursed her lips and nodded sagely, as if she understood that some subjects were too tender for words.

"With all your success, do you ever still feel like that little runt who was always getting picked on?" Though she'd asked about him, he knew the hurt little kid she worried about was herself.

Damn, he wanted to toss out a glib response about how he'd buried that pathetic kid decades ago and never thought twice about him anymore, but the raw emotion in her voice and the way her teeth gnawed on her lower lip made it impossible for him to be anything less than truthful.

"As much as I wish I could tell you that my adult successes have vanquished my inner runt, I can't. The poor squirt still pops up every now and then."

She released a heavy breath and picked up her sandwich again, but didn't take a bite. "That's what I was afraid of."

Half an hour later, Shayna feared her nerves would burst through her skin as she stared at the wintry outlook. Zero percent chance of sunshine for the next two days, a fifty-fifty chance the temperature would creep above freezing sometime Friday afternoon.

The news ended and a car commercial blasted out of her little set. She lowered the volume and twisted on the couch, facing the comfy blue recliner where Kyle sat, the ice pack once again covering his wound.

Seeing him like that threw her mind and her body back

to those scorching few minutes in the kitchen. The sight of him sprawled out at her table, looking as if he belonged, had scrambled her brain. For a second she'd forgotten who he was and why he was here. All she'd been able to think about was curling up against that broad, strong chest and kissing the daylights out of him.

Clearing her throat, she nodded toward the whispering television. "It doesn't look good."

"It didn't sound good." He sat up and laid the ice pack on the coffee table, next to the pieces of her soon-to-be less revealing Ms. Noel costume. "Exactly how long will we be stuck up here, away from civilization?"

"Assuming it doesn't rain again, just until Saturday." She plucked up her costume and her sewing kit and settled back into the couch cushions. She needed to get the sleeves and hem tacked up so she could attach the faux fur trim tomorrow.

"*Saturday?* But the guy said the temp would rise above forty Friday afternoon. Surely the ice'll melt off the road by then."

"Yeah, but by then, the icy road won't be the main problem. We won't be able to get back to town till the bridge over Shiner's Gulch thaws, and that's going to take above-freezing temps *and* sunshine."

"You're telling me a little bad weather and no one can get up or down this blasted mountain. What about emergencies?"

"Usually, if the bridge is impassable, we can get to town the back way, but…well, there was an accident about two miles up the road a few weeks back. Highway department hasn't gotten it repaired yet."

Her cheeks warmed as Kyle flashed her a steely look that she bet had caused many a dishonest witness to crumble. "What kind of accident?"

"An explosion. Sort of."

"Sort of? An explosion is usually one of those things that very definitely is or isn't. Which was it?"

Drat! She dropped the costume to her lap. Did the man have to cross-examine everything?

"It was a definite *accidental* explosion." When she noticed her fingers fidgeting in her hair, she paused, drew a deep breath and forced her hands back into her lap. She would not squirm like a sinner on Sunday.

"Mr. McGuffy goofed his recipe and his still blew up. It landed in the middle of the road. The stuff was so high proof that it burned hot enough to melt the asphalt. Now there's a giant sinkhole in the middle of the road that you can't drive around."

"Moonshine?" he asked incredulously.

"Yep. It's an old tradition in these parts, a teenaged right of passage, sneaking up the mountain to Mr. McGuffy's. It's usually harmless fun, but I'm afraid the tradition is officially over now."

"I should think so. Do the parents know what's going on?"

She snickered, totally entertained by his reactions. "Oh, yeah. Most of the people who grew up around here have more than their fair share of McGuffy stories."

"What about you? I'd imagine living this close you were a frequent customer."

She shook her head, her stomach turning queasy at the memory. "I only did it once. The year I turned twelve, I tagged along with some older friends. Two couples. I wasn't really there for the shine, but about halfway through our jar, they become more interested in kissing, so I finished the stuff off by myself. I was sick as a dog for three straight days."

"At that age, you're lucky you didn't get alcohol poisoning."

"Yeah, that's what Daddy told me. The next day, he made me work in the yard—in the hot sun—all day. I spent hours puking and pulling weeds."

Lines crinkled around his eyes, and his dimple danced as he laughed. "Bet you learned your lesson."

"Darn tooting I did. To this day, I'm not a big drinker. And I never go along with something just because everyone else does."

"Sometimes the hardest learned lessons are the best," he remarked.

She shimmied deeper into the couch cushions, a wicked grin splitting her face, surprised to realize she was enjoying Kyle's company. "That sounds like the voice of experience. Let's hear it."

Well, hell. This woman sure knew how to turn a simple conversation into a verbal mine field.

Getting Shayna to drop her guard was one thing, but revisiting his own miserable childhood was another. Still, they were bonding, and even though he hated swapping personal tidbits, if it helped get the job done, Kyle would force himself to bite the bullet.

He cleared his throat. "I'm afraid most of my life experiences aren't fit for sharing in mixed company."

"Sooo you were a bad boy, huh?"

"You could say that." His father sure as hell must have thought so, considering how often the old man smacked him around.

"Come on, you've got to share. It's only fair. What's the worst thing you did as a kid?"

"Are you saying getting smashed on moonshine was the worst thing *you've* ever done?"

"Not the worst," she admitted vaguely, her lids lowering

to hide her expressive amber eyes. "But it definitely taught me several lessons I've never forgotten. Surely you pulled some kind of stunt as a kid that still affects you today?"

Had he ever. His list of past mistakes was long and personal and something he never talked about. Ever.

"I almost got arrested for armed robbery when I was fifteen." The confession stunned him nearly as much as it did her.

"Almost?" Eyes wide open now, she leaned intently toward him and hugged her arms around herself. "Sounds like you caught a break."

"Yeah, not that I was very grateful at the time." But in the end, that near miss had started him thinking about getting out, about finding a way to turn his life around before he ended up just like his old man.

Shayna didn't respond, but something about the patient, nonjudgmental way she watched him made him want to share the details, to explain, as she had, the way he'd turned a negative experience into a positive life lesson.

"Back then, my family life really sucked, so I'd started hanging out with a neighborhood gang after school rather than going back to whatever crisis had erupted at home."

His foster parents at the time had an affinity for off-track betting. When their horse failed to show, they liked to take their frustration out on the first kid through the door.

"One day, the leader of our sorry gang decided we should hang out at the local Cash 'N' Go. Seemed I was the only one who didn't know they planned to rob the place. At gunpoint."

"Oh, no." Her worried cry mingled with the popping fire reminded him they were completely alone. The solitude made it easier to speak the truth.

"Yeah. When I realized what was up, I pretended to trip over a potato chip display. The distraction caught the clerk's attention and he ran us off. The guys beat the crap out of me every day for a week, but at least I didn't end up with a criminal record."

Warily, Kyle lifted his eyes to hers. Where he'd feared revulsion or censure, he found understanding and admiration. It was a humbling combination.

"You did the right thing."

"I know that now, but back then, when I was nursing cracked ribs, I was sure it was the stupidest move I'd ever made."

"You were only fifteen. I'd be willing to bet you've done a ton of more stupid things since then."

Amazingly, her teasing soothed his lingering discomfort over exposing the details of his past. How the devil could one woman be so easy to talk to one minute and so damned difficult the next?

"You would definitely win that bet."

"See, that wasn't so bad now, was it?" She tapped his knee before relaxing back against the cushion. "A little more practice and I'm sure you'll conquer your fear of social chitchat." With a teasing wink, she lightened the mood, but the damage was done. He'd set out to get her to lower her guard, and instead, she'd completely turned the tables on him.

"I think swapping childhood stupidities goes beyond the scope of mere social chitchat."

"Guess that means we've exceeded expectations, huh? And for our reward—a movie. Two straight hours, no talking necessary."

"What movie?"

"Home Alone." She smirked, looking as young and innocent as the child star from the movie, who, if memory served, turned out to be a hell-raiser in real life.

"The movie with the little blond kid who kicks butt against a couple of criminals?"

"That's the one. And no fair rooting for the bad guys."

"Who, me? I'm all about justice."

"No, you're all about rich clients and good PR." As soon as the words were out, she cringed, obviously wishing she could take them back, but since *she'd* broached the subject, he figured the ground rules no longer held. It was the opportunity he'd been waiting for and he couldn't afford to waste it.

"Who says justice and public relations have to be mutually exclusive?"

All her humor and lightheartedness instantly retreated. "Surely you don't honestly believe Walker's offer has anything to do with justice? He's just trying to buy back his credibility."

"And isn't that a form of justice? Admitting to past mistakes and taking steps to rectify them?"

"How can it be true justice without punishment—on his part?"

Warming to the topic, Kyle leaned forward, his hands resting on his knees. "He's offering to pay you a million dollars. That kind of a fine sounds like steep punishment to me."

"It's not a fine when he insists on getting something in exchange."

"What he's asking for won't cost you anything but a little of your time."

Her spine went rigid, giving her small frame an impressive air of power that almost overshadowed the shimmer of tears in her expressive amber eyes. "What about my integrity? My self-respect? My *daddy's* reputation? If I accept Walker's guilt money, I'll lose all of those."

"Shayna, I know it's hard, but you can't look at this situation emotionally." He softened his tone, wanting to soothe rather than agitate. "It's a business deal, pure and simple, and it benefits everyone involved."

"What about you? How do you benefit?"

"This isn't about me. I've simply been hired to execute the paperwork."

She eyed him shrewdly. "But you have a vested interest in seeing that things work out in Walker's favor."

"Yes."

"More than just a vested interest, I'd say, if you followed me halfway across the country. What's in this for you?"

Under normal circumstances, Kyle would never discuss his personal stakes, but these weren't normal circumstances. "Dr. Walker is one of our firm's most influential clients. Handling this case is my final step to making partner."

"Aren't you kind of young to be a partner?"

"I'll be the youngest by ten years, but I've worked my entire life to earn the honor. It's all I've ever wanted, and I'm very determined when it comes to achieving my goals."

"Determined enough to align yourself with manipulative, dishonest people like Dr. Walker?"

He opened his mouth, not sure if he planned to defend Walker or himself, but she cut him off.

"Never mind. I can't talk about this anymore tonight." She clutched the bundle of red fabric and stood. "I think I'll call it a day."

Ordinarily, at this point in a debate, with his opponent so obviously on the ropes, Kyle would force the issue and seize victory. Tonight, however, with Shayna, he couldn't stomach the idea of kicking her while she was down.

"But it's only seven-thirty."

"I guess I'm more tired than I thought." The slump in

her shoulders and the lines between her brows spoke more of weariness than sleepiness.

"What about the movie?" he asked, suddenly desperate for her to stay and relax. He wanted to see the joy return to her face.

A wistful look flashed across her face. "It is one of my favorites."

"Then don't go. No more shoptalk tonight. I promise."

Her eyebrows twitched, her doubt a tangible force in the room. "Then whatever will we talk about?"

He heard the flicker of humor return to her voice. Not bothering to fight back his grin, he gestured to the sofa. "So, what's the deal with the ball of red fabric?"

Her look of relief was almost comical. "It's my costume for the upcoming Noel Festival. I'm Ms. Noel."

"So you're the star of the show?"

She eased back down on the sofa, favoring him with a tentative smile before feeding a length of red thread through a needle. "More like head volunteer. Ms. Noel serves as hostess for all the festival's fundraising events."

"Ah, local Christmas traditions. Definite social chitchat kind of stuff. Tell me more."

"Wellll." She drew the word out, her lips puckering as if she were shooting him a kiss across the room. "Everything kicks off Saturday night with the Junior Miss Noel Pageant. Ms. Noel serves as the master of ceremonies. Then Sunday is the countywide toy drive."

"Will the weather clear up enough for you to make both events?"

"If it doesn't, I'll just have to hike back to town. Can't have the Noel Festival without Ms. Noel." Her fingers flew over the dress's edge.

"That's some pretty powerful optimism you have there."

"What's the alternative? Walk around expecting the worst? That's no fun."

"Life isn't always about having fun," he pointed out.

"Trust me, I'm well aware of that. But what have you got to lose by choosing sunshine over gloom and doom?"

He leaned back in his chair, his fingers linked across his chest. "Nothing, I guess, but being prepared helps mitigate the damage when the inevitable gloom and doom hits."

Shayna rolled here eyes. "No, it doesn't. Sitting around waiting for bad things to happen doesn't make them any less horrible. It just makes life miserable all the time."

"So you're saying we should skip around whistling a happy tune all the time and ignore reality?"

"I'm saying we should skip and whistle whenever we can, so we have happy memories to fight for when trouble comes. If you don't treasure the sunshine, why even bother fighting against the gloom and doom?"

Damn good thing it was a rhetorical question, because Kyle, whose life had been sorely lacking in sunshine, sure as hell didn't have an answer.

Chapter Five

After a night of too much thinking and too little sleeping, Kyle finally crawled out of bed around 8:00 a.m. For the first time in his career, his objectivity was slipping.

Shayna was getting to him, working her way around his emotional shields, tempting him to care. She'd even gotten him to break his cardinal rule against talking about his past.

He had to put an end to this growing connection, had to find a way to keep her firmly in the opposition role, to stop seeing her as a desirable, intriguing woman he wanted to spend a week in bed with.

His body sprung to full attention at the idea of a naked, sleepy Shayna in his bed. "Holy hell." He threw back the covers and sat up, rubbing a hand over his face. Never in his life had he been this affected by one particular woman, and he damned sure didn't like it.

The cabin was dead quiet when he opened the bedroom

door. A weak, ashy light strained through the sheer curtains, signaling what he assumed was this morning's lack of sunshine. In the kitchen, he found the coffeemaker set and ready to go. All he had to do was push the green button and wait.

The heady scent of morning brew gave a few of his brain cells a head start. Behind him, he heard a click-clack and turned just in time for Brinks to jump on his chest rather than his back. He staggered under the dog's weight.

In place of last night's toothy scowl, the beast wore what could only be described as a grin. His tail wagged fast enough to power a small country.

"Good morning, Dr. Jekyll. I met your alter ego last night."

The dog woofed, then jumped down and made a beeline for the back door. Understanding the urgency, Kyle let him out. A thin sheet of ice coated everything. Both his and Brinks's breath turned to steam in the frigid morning air.

Under different circumstances, he might find the scene beautiful. The world looked clean and calm. But today, he didn't want clean and calm. He wanted to wrap things up and be on his way. He needed to get back to his world, to claim his partnership and move forward with his life.

Back inside, the coffeemaker dinged. Kyle called the dog and they hustled inside. With his first, vital cup of coffee in hand, he began pacing the quiet confines of Shayna's home.

His brain spun at warp speed, contemplating how to turn this roadblock into his advantage. He had to find a way to capitalize on having Shayna's undivided attention, because by God, when the roads and bridges cleared, he *would* have his life and his career back on track.

Thinking of the bridge reminded him of last night's accident and the e-mail he hadn't gotten to read. Anticipating the key to getting this job done, he stalked back into his room and dug his cell phone out of his briefcase. He flipped open the phone. Good battery, zero reception. Damn.

He quickly layered on all the dry clothing he had, both his and hers, and after stuffing the phone in his pocket, headed for the front yard to hunt for an active cell signal. He jerked the sweatshirt's hood over his head and carefully navigated his way across her front yard. Frozen grass crunched beneath his feet like broken glass.

The bars on his phone popped up, then died away again as he took another step. He backed up and quickly opened his inbox. He had several other messages waiting, but at the moment, he was only interested in reading Amanda's report.

No adoption records for the minor Shayna Hoyt.

Checked birth certificate files and found one in Mass for Shayna Hoyt, father unknown, and another in Tenn, same dates and vitals, listing father as James Miller. Patricia Hoyt listed as mother in both records.

Kyle reread the message twice.

Damn. No wonder she didn't want Dr. Walker outed as her birth father. If the truth were revealed, Shayna Miller would cease to exist, because duplicate birth certificates could mean only one thing: one was forged. And if James Miller had forged Shayna's birth certificate, that meant he'd never been legally granted permanent custody of her when she was seven, as they'd both claimed.

This was what he'd been waiting on. The key to Shayna's cooperation, the ammunition he needed to get this case wrapped up quickly.

Heart heavy, Kyle returned the phone to his pocket and turned back toward the house.

So where the hell was his usual rush of victory?

* * *

She'd overslept. A very rare occurrence. Normally, Brinks's bladder was more reliable than any alarm clock. Shayna rolled over and stretched her legs toward the foot of the bed, feeling around for the dog.

Nothing but heavy covers and cool sheets. Prying her eyelids open, she squinted at the murky light filling her room. Wow. She'd *really* overslept.

Throwing off the covers, she sat up and dropped her bare feet to the floor. A whistle flew from her lips as she immediately yanked her warm toes off the icy hardwood. Thinking longingly of the thick socks she'd dropped on Kyle's bed last night, she hopped up and scurried to the bathroom, where her slippers waited. When she'd finished up in the bathroom and returned to her room, she found Brinks sprawled across her bed.

"Good morning, handsome. Thanks for letting me sleep in."

The big old softie rolled over and showed her his belly. Unable to resist, she complied with his silent request. His coarse fur was freezing. Looked as if her guest had his good points after all.

"Did you thank Kyle for letting you out?"

The dog barked in response and raced back downstairs. Shayna followed, much more slowly, wishing she shared a smidge of the dog's enthusiasm for the coming day.

Last night had not gone according to plan.

First was the off-the-chart surge of lust, where she'd nearly attacked him at the dinner table. Honestly, she didn't know what had gotten into her. It's not as if he was the first good-looking man she'd met. So why did this man—so determined to stir up things she wanted to forget—pack such a wallop?

Then he'd opened up, shared details about his life she

was sure he generally kept close to the vest. That glimpse of vulnerability made him even more attractive to her.

Still, she'd nearly gotten the evening back on track, then—bam!—before she knew what had happened, they'd been hip deep in a discussion about Walker, the very thing she'd sworn to avoid.

She hadn't been in any kind of shape mentally to tackle that subject, and Kyle had knocked her for another loop when he'd offered a cease-fire rather than deliver a crushing verbal blow.

Talk about a welcome surprise.

Downstairs, the invigorating aroma of fresh coffee filled the cabin. She trod quietly into the den, her glance taking in the open door to the spare room.

"Kyle?"

The bathroom that connected to his room had a door that opened directly into the main room, and it was open, as well. Where the devil was he? She hoped he hadn't tried to walk back down the road in those slippery leather shoes of his. He was likely to break his fool neck.

Worried, she started to rush to the mudroom for her boots, but a dark shape caught her attention through the front window. Shayna inched closer and saw Kyle, standing in the middle of the front yard, hunched against the wind, the hood of her old sweatshirt pulled over his head, his BlackBerry held a few inches in front of his nose.

Amazed that he'd found a signal, she headed for the kitchen and the waiting coffee. Brinks laid sprawled in front of the refrigerator, his favorite spot downstairs. According to the coffeemaker, it was a quarter past nine. Shayna fixed herself a cup and headed through the mudroom, pulling on her toasty work coat and slipping her feet into her heavy boots before stepping out on the back porch.

Brinks flew past her, making a mad dash for some unseen critter in the woods.

She could see the wind blowing through the trees, but the three-sided porch protected her from the blast. Apparently, a corner of her brain had been hoping the weatherman had made a mistake, but the heavy, gray clouds and the icicle lawn proved he'd gotten it right.

Hands huddled around her steaming mug, she let her gaze wander over the yard. In the far corner, her garden drooped under the damaging ice. Those veggies were vital to making her budget stretch. She couldn't afford to lose the whole lot to bad weather.

Grabbing an empty bushel basket, she carefully picked her way across the slippery lawn. The frost stung her bare fingers as she harvested the last of her fall produce. Eggplant, carrots, broccoli, onions, a few wrinkled bell peppers, and a good mess of beans. Since they weren't expecting a hard freeze, she left the potatoes tucked in the earth.

Hope Kyle doesn't mind a vegetable cornucopia for Thanksgiving dinner. Though she did have a ham and some frozen garden veggies in the freezer…and she knew she had all the ingredients for green bean casserole. That was supposed to be her contribution to dinner at Lindy's.

Shoot! She needed to call and let Lindy know she was fine and dandy but wouldn't make Thanksgiving. She whistled for Brinks. The dog came running, his tongue hanging out of lips that she'd have sworn were smiling.

On her way back inside, she stopped and rummaged through the freezer, unearthing an eight-pound ham. The frozen meat burned her fingers, and she dashed over and dropped their main course in the sink. Grabbing the phone with one hand and stoppering the sink with the other,

Shayna glanced out the window behind the table. Kyle still stood in the same spot, in the same position.

Once she had the ham covered, she turned off the water and dialed Lindy's number. Travis answered on the second ring.

"Hey, Shayna. How's the weather up there?"

"Perfect, if you like icy and isolated."

"We were afraid you'd be stuck."

"Well, I haven't tried the roads yet, but judging by last night's rain and this morning's temps—" not to mention her guest's eyewitness account "—I'm pretty sure the bridge'll be an icy mess."

"Are you okay up there? Got everything you need?" It was so like Travis to ask.

"I'll be fine. The propane tank's full, and I just picked a whole bushel of vegetables. It might not be a traditional Thanksgiving, but we'll survive."

She crinkled her eyes at her accidental use of the plural pronoun, but Travis must have assumed she meant her and the dog, because he didn't comment. They exchanged holiday wishes before he handed the phone off to his wife.

"I knew you should have spent the night with us."

"Then Brinks would be iced in all by himself. I couldn't let that happen." She carried the portable phone over to the fireplace and began poking at the embers. "Besides, it's not like we're going to die up here. It's just a couple of days, and I've already assured Travis we have all the basic necessities covered."

"Good. But you're going to miss dinner with the family."

Shayna could hear the tears welling in her friend's voice. Pregnancy hormones had turned Lindy into a drop-of-the-hat crier.

She stuck the phone between her chin and shoulder and muscled a couple logs into the fireplace. "The ice should melt in time for me to drop by for leftovers in a few days, and that's my favorite part anyway."

Lindy sniffled. "Okay."

Just then, the front door pushed open. Shayna covered the mouthpiece with her hand and stood. Kyle reentered the cabin, a blast of cold air sneaking in with him, blowing through the cabin and fanning the flames Shayna was stoking.

Barely aware of Lindy's voice in her ear, Shayna stared as he pushed the hood off his head. His sapphire eyes darkened as they focused on her lips. Staring at him, she had to remind herself to breathe. A cowlick stuck out from the top of his blond head, and his face was as red as a child in a Norman Rockwell Christmas print. But despite his cherubic look, he was all man, and her body knew it.

"Shayna!" Lindy's high-pitched voice reclaimed Shayna's lost attention.

"Sorry. What?" She backed up and rested her bottom on the arm of the couch as Kyle moved next to her, holding his wide, strong hands out toward the heat of the fire.

"I said, I wish you weren't spending your holiday alone."

"I'm not alone." The truthful answer was instinctive, but when Kyle's head whipped in her direction, his left eyebrow cocked into a question mark, she began to second-guess herself.

She didn't want to lie, but if Lindy knew she was stranded up here with a man she barely knew, Lindy would freak out. Shayna hated the idea of adding to her stress, especially since there wasn't anything her pregnant friend could do about the situation.

Besides, given her unprecedented physical reaction, it was best no one knew about his short visit, especially her best friend, who had a tendency to see more than Shayna wanted her to.

"What do you mean 'not alone'?" Lindy asked.

"Well, I've got Brinks to keep me company." Warmth that had nothing to do with the fire flushed Shayna's skin. She wanted to turn her back and ignore her guest, but instead, she leveled her gaze at him.

He shrugged one shoulder and returned his attention to the fire.

"Oh, you and that dog." Lindy's exasperated sigh was interrupted by the muffled sound of Travis's voice in the background. "Looks like I've gotta go."

"Oh, you and that husband," Shayna teased.

"Damn right. I can only hope one day—one day soon—you find a man who outranks even Brinks."

"Me, too," Shayna told her friend.

She thumbed the off button and cradled the phone in her lap. In her periphery, she saw Kyle's body swivel as he sat on the hearth, his back to the fire. The warm glow played through his hair like sunshine.

"Ashamed to tell your friends about me?"

If only it were that simple. "Of course not. Lindy's pregnant, and I didn't want her to worry about me being stuck up here with a potential lunatic."

"Potential? So the jury's still out?" His lips curled, crinkling his dimple to life.

Sitting in the beam of that sexy smile, her blood warmed, delicious tingles zinging to all her sensitive places. "I believe I'll plead the fifth."

"I thought you were all about social chitchatting?"

"Oh, I am, but I also believe a woman's entitled to her

secrets." Hyperaware of just how close Kyle's body was to hers, she sprung to her feet. He rose too, his nearness effectively pinning her in place.

His fingers brushed the hair out of her face and tucked it behind her ear. "Careful, Shayna." The deep timbre of his voice pulsated beneath her skin. "Uncovering a woman's secrets is a temptation most men can't resist."

Shayna's focus was riveted on his firm lips as he spoke. Would his kiss be tentative and tender or demanding and devastating?

Forcibly reminding herself that she had too much at stake to risk finding out, she sidestepped around him. "Thanks for the warning. A girl can never be too careful."

Shayna dillydallied in her room for as long as she dared. She dressed, deciding on her favorite jeans (the magical ones that made her look like she had long legs) and her new orange silk-and-cashmere blend sweater. Telling herself it was all about the holiday spirit, she put a little extra effort into her makeup and ditched her regular braid in favor of a softer twist.

She didn't know what irked her more—that she'd lied about his presence or that Kyle had called her on it. She honestly hadn't wanted to risk upsetting Lindy, but more than anything, she didn't want everyone and their brother to find out she'd been stranded with Kyle.

It wouldn't take long for tongues to start wagging. Her neighbors would speculate about them entertaining themselves horizontally, even though Shayna had never been the casual fling type. But truth be told, had Kyle been stranded here for any other reason, goodness knew the speculation would have been dead-on. She wanted that irritating man something fierce.

If she didn't find some way to establish stronger boundaries, she would likely become so distracted by her attraction that Kyle could talk her into anything.

Rising worry propelled her into action. She had to get control of her rampant hormones. The next forty-eight hours were critical. She had to stay focused, she had to maintain a safe distance and mostly, she had to find a way to get Kyle—and Walker—out of her life. Pronto.

How the heck would she accomplish such a monumental task? First, no more mooning over her sexy houseguest. That would lead to nothing but trouble, and she certainly didn't need any more of that.

Step two, figure out how the heck to turn down Walker's crazy proposal and cut all ties with him and Patty.

Easy as pie, right?

While she waited for inspiration to strike, she'd just have to march down there, park Kyle in front of the football games and sequester herself in the kitchen.

Not the greatest game plan, but somehow, she'd have to make it work. Grabbing her nearly finished Ms. Noel costume, she headed downstairs, delightfully surprised by the roaring fire and the scrumptious aroma of sautéing onions. The rattle of pots and pans led her to the kitchen, where she found Kyle standing at the stove, his back to her. Brinks noticed her presence first and raced over, calling her to the man's attention. He turned, his face flushed from the heat of the stove.

His eyes slowly roamed up and down her body. Feeling more exposed than she had last night in her gaping robe, she forced herself to stand steady under his heated regard, despite the heavy warmth invading her belly. She had to keep these blasted reactions hidden or he'd pounce like a mountain lion feasting on a scared rabbit.

"Nice." A muscle trembled along his whiskery jawline as he turned back to the sizzling pan.

That single, soft-spoken syllable affected Shayna more than a bucketful of flowery words ever could. She had to lick her suddenly parched lips before she could respond. "Thanks."

She dropped her hand onto Brinks's head and rubbed behind his ears. His liquid brown eyes stared up at her. One side of his mouth was hooked on his teeth. The look seemed to say, "Go on. I've got your back."

Putting on her game face, Shayna tossed the costume onto the table and headed for the sink. "You look like an old pro in here," she commented as she washed her hands.

He shrugged. The movement's forced nonchalance reminded her of the foster care children she worked with at the County Community Center. They craved praise and encouragement but got it so rarely that when they did they rejected it. "I've been cooking since I was a teenager."

"Did your mother teach you?"

"No," he said bitterly. "She wasn't what you'd call the domestic type."

Again, she was taken aback by the reminder that she'd so misjudged his background. The man had done an awesome job of washing away all the visible signs of his less than stellar childhood. "So where'd you learn?"

"In high school, I worked nights at a greasy diner." With a smooth flick of his wrist, he slid slices of the bell peppers she'd picked this morning into the sizzling pan. "By the time I got to college, I had landed a position as line cook at a posh supper club."

She could easily picture him maturing, both in age and in skill, and working his way up the food-service ladder. Guess he came by that bulldog determination naturally.

"Lucky me, getting stranded with a man who can cook," she joked, wanting to steer clear of the past. Very dangerous territory. "So, what's on the menu?"

"Corn chowder, broccoli and rice, beer bread, baked apples, ham and green bean casserole."

"Sounds yummy. And complicated. And way beyond the capabilities of me and my poor neglected pantry."

"All those fresh vegetables are the key. And I found all kinds of good stuff in the freezer. Your green thumb has saved the day." His lips curled, his eyes twinkled, his delicious dimple teased. The look was pure charm.

Good. Charisma she could handle. It was the notion that he'd try to get at her with honest commiseration that she worried about.

"So, what can I do to help?"

Kyle turned off the gas under the skillet and moved it to a back burner before turning, his face comically contorted into a mask of outraged alarm. "You do know Thanksgiving dinner requires actual cooking, right?"

Jeez. Why did he have to be so darn likable?

Laughing, she jabbed his arm. "Very funny. I'm not completely useless in the kitchen. I can certainly follow a recipe."

"I'm sure you can, but for today, I'm banning you from the kitchen."

"But it's *my* kitchen."

He spread his arms, indicating the groceries and cooking gear covering the counter space. "I plan to trade a home-cooked Thanksgiving dinner for my room and board. All you have to do is relax and let me do all the work." His dimple flared to life.

"Said the spider to the fly."

"Don't you trust me?"

"Not one lick, buster."

"Well, I could let you cook and just write you a check to cover my expenses, but I figured that would piss you off." His dimple beamed even brighter, and she had to fight back a grin of her own.

She knew his offer was a beguiling trap. Nothing with this man was as simple as it sounded, but honestly, it was hard to see the downside of having a good-looking guy cook you a lavish meal.

"Do you promise to behave?"

He held his fingers aloft in a two-fingered salute. "Scout's honor."

"Were you really a Boy Scout?"

"What do you think?"

"I think this is going to be a very interesting day."

"Does that mean we have a deal?"

"Yeah. You cook and I'll clean." She extended her hand. His large, warm palm swallowed hers. Unlike the first time they'd shaken hands, at the ground breaking ceremony, this time Shayna's skin wasn't insulated by gloves. The shock of skin on skin contact shot a bolt of electricity up her arm, sending a river of wet heat straight to her core.

"Deal." He withdrew his hand, his thumb dragging slowly and sensuously across the sensitive skin of her palm. His Adam's apple bobbed twice. "Now scram, or we'll end up going to bed hungry."

She nodded and backed out of the narrow space, stopping only long enough to retrieve her costume. As she plopped herself on the sofa, a safe distance from the lust storm raging in the kitchen, Shayna figured she'd be going to bed hungry tonight, no matter how much food Kyle prepared.

The man had stirred a craving in her that she feared she'd never satisfy.

Chapter Six

After two straight hours of cooking, Kyle's body still hungered for a taste of Shayna. He slid the casserole dish into the oven, fighting the urge to slam the oven door.

Normally, he found cooking a great stress-reducer, but with erotic images of Shayna filling his brain, he couldn't find his usual peace. Perhaps if he didn't keep catching glimpses of her curled up in the corner of the sofa, firelight sparking blond highlights to life in her luxurious hair, the tip of her pink tongue captured between her perfectly white teeth as she stretched and smoothed a portion of red velvet across her lap.

His body grew hard and tight. Damn, but this woman packed an unwelcome punch. He'd come to Tennessee to get a job done, not compromise his professional ethics, but being around Shayna made it nearly impossible to keep his mind on business.

Earlier, when they'd shaken hands, the spark had nearly short-circuited his brain. All he'd been able to think of was pulling her body against his and tasting those luscious, shimmering lips.

Who the hell was he kidding? He'd wanted to strip off her skintight jeans and make love to her on the kitchen table.

Hell of a way to earn her trust.

Damn it. Earning her trust wasn't supposed to be a part of the plan.

Finding out about Shayna's dual birth certificates gave Kyle a hell of an advantage, and he should be planning how and when to use the information. No only did it strengthen his client's position but it also added teeth to Patty's more nefarious claims, which until this morning, he'd thought preposterous.

Now he wasn't so sure.

He knew from experience that delaying bad news only made it more difficult to deliver. And to receive. The situation called for swift, decisive action, but every strategy he came up with felt heartless and cruel.

Bottom line was he'd lost his objectivity and with it, his edge. He found himself worrying more about sparing Shayna than serving his client. Definite career suicide.

"Hey." Shayna cautiously entered into the kitchen. "Care for some company? All this silence is getting on my nerves." She pulled out a chair and sat facing into the kitchen.

Seeing her so close to the scene of his recent fantasy rattled him. How much temptation was one man expected to resist?

Trying to maintain his cool by focusing on the familiar routines of cooking, he grabbed the pan of boiled eggs and drained the water into the sink. "Aren't you used to the quiet?"

"Usually it doesn't bother me, but today's a holiday and that's different."

"How?"

"You know." She shrugged as if the answer should be obvious. "Holidays mean lots of friends and family, tons of talking and laughing and gossiping and catching up. Not having all that makes me really miss my family. Surely, spending the holiday away from your home, you can understand how I feel."

The boiled egg he'd been in the process of shelling oozed through his tightly fisted fingers. "I don't have much contact with my family anymore."

"Sorry to hear that." Genuine regret laced her voice. "So how do you normally spend the holiday?"

"Scooping dressing at a local homeless shelter." He felt a pang of regret for leaving the mission hanging. He knew from personal experience how demanding hungry kids could be. Volunteers were always at a premium for the annual holiday feast, and he knew that even if his face wouldn't be missed, his hands certainly would.

"That's great. My daddy always said sharing your blessings with others feeds the soul and keeps good things coming your way."

"In California, we call that karma."

"In Tennessee, we call it being good people." Cautiously, she edged farther into the kitchen and poured herself a glass of iced tea. "So do you cook, too, or just serve?"

"Are you kidding? It would take me a year to make enough cornbread dressing to feed thousands."

"But you send a check, don't you? Probably anonymously, right?"

Amazed that she'd once again pegged him, he shrugged

as he finished dicing the last egg. "I'm always looking for year-end tax deductions."

"Bull. You donate money and volunteer your time because you, Kyle Anderson, are good people, no matter how hard you try to hide it." Rather than returning to the table, she leaned against the edge of the counter.

"Don't paint me as a hero too quickly. After the shelter, I spend the rest of the long weekend at the office. It's amazing how much you can accomplish when no one's around to interrupt."

"You work on Thanksgiving? That's so sad."

"It gives me an edge. I told you I'm determined to make partner." He covered the chopped eggs and washed his hands. Tired of struggling with his conscience, he decided to try another tack. If he could convince her to cooperate with Walker's plan, there'd be no reason to expose James Miller's secrets.

"Speaking of sharing your blessings, I've been thinking about this Noel Festival and the money you're hoping to raise for the youth center. A million dollars would buy a ton of books and basketballs."

Her face paled and her posture stiffened, but she didn't glance away. "It certainly would, and the center would be thrilled to receive such a large donation, but it won't be coming from me. At least not by way of Dr. Walker's guilt money."

"I know you hate him, but he is your biological father. You are entitled to a share of his estate. He wants to see that you get what you deserve."

"What I deserve?" Her voice got louder and her drawl thickened. "Do I deserve to be publicly humiliated just so your client can cover his own ass?"

"Walker doesn't deny making mistakes in the past—

huge mistakes. But he can't make amends without your cooperation."

"This isn't about him making amends. It's about ensuring his stellar public image remains untarnished by the truth."

Brinks lifted his head from his paws and perked his ears before standing up. With an indignant groan, he left the kitchen. Apparently their argument was disturbing the dog's nap.

Not wanting this conversation to escalate into another shouting match, he lowered his voice to a near-whisper. "Have you ever considered that he's trying to do now what he couldn't do then? When you were born, he was just starting his career. He was struggling. Perhaps now that he's financially secure, he wants to give you what he couldn't before."

"Bull. If he honestly wanted to compensate me for all those years of neglect, he wouldn't have attached such ridiculous strings to the money."

"I'm not saying the man's a saint, but Patty has now forced him to handle matters publicly. If the money is transferred silently, she can still threaten exposure. Wouldn't you prefer this secret be brought to light under Walker's control rather than Patty's?"

"I'd prefer for this matter to disappear altogether."

"Shayna, no matter what happened in the past, you are his daughter. The money is your birthright. Does it really matter what his motives are?"

"Yes, it matters. If he's looking for absolution, I can't give him that. Ever." She crossed her arms over her chest, her stance becoming defensive and distrustful.

Kyle gripped the counter's edge behind him to keep from reaching out and cradling her against his chest. As much as he hated to admit it, the kindest thing he could do for her right now was drop the whole load of crap at once, like a bad-news bomb. The damage would be quick and severe, but once the wounds healed, she'd be able to deal with everything and move on.

"Shayna, are you aware that Walker isn't the only one Patty's threatening to expose?"

She squinted warily. "Does she have something on you, too?"

"No. Your dad."

Her eyelids closed, and she nodded in resignation. "What's she saying?" she asked softly.

"She claims he kidnapped you and that she never went to the police because he threatened to kill you if she did."

Her eyes went as wide and round as silver dollars, fierce despite the shine of tears. "That's not true!"

"Shayna, you were only seven. How can you be sure?"

"Because I was there."

"Unfortunately, my secretary e-mailed me information this morning that seems to support Patty's claims." No longer able to resist his need to comfort her, he cupped his hands around her trembling shoulders. "There's no record of an adoption, yet you have his name."

"It's not illegal to change your name."

"No, but it is illegal for one person to have two birth certificates."

Tears clung to her lower lids, but she somehow kept them from falling. "They wouldn't let me enroll in school without one."

"So he forged one?"

"Yes, but I swear that's the one and only time we ever broke the law."

"He took a child he didn't have legal custody of across state lines, Shayna. That's a very serious crime."

"He did have custody. CPS assigned him as my temporary guardian because Patty was in jail."

"If he had court-approved custody, then why did he forge your documentation?"

"He called the Boston Social Service offices several times, trying to get copies of the court records, but they were so swamped, it was weeks before he even spoke to an actual caseworker, and she couldn't locate my file. School had already started, so he had the fake birth certificate made. It was supposed to be a temporary fix. We didn't expect the move to be permanent."

"Why did he bring you to Tennessee in the first place?"

"A couple of days after they awarded him custody, his grandfather, who'd raised him, got sick. We went to the prison and told Patty where we were going and why. James gave her Papa Joe's phone number and told her to call when she got her act together, but she never did. After that first year, we realized she probably wasn't ever coming back, but by then, the whole town had accepted us as father and daughter. It would have been too confusing and too difficult to tell the truth at that point."

She finally lost her battle against the tears. A single drop fell against her cheek. Kyle raised his hands to her face, using his thumbs to wipe away the moisture.

"We didn't hurt anybody," she continued, sadness making her voice gravelly. "Patty obviously didn't want me, and at that time she'd told me my birth father wasn't even in the picture. In the end, what we did was best for everyone. The county—who must have never found my missing file because we never heard from them—had one less unwanted kid to deal with, Papa Joe had his son around to take care of him in his final days and I finally had a family. How can that be wrong?"

"I'm afraid that what's right and what's legal aren't always the same thing. And in this case, even though Miller's intentions were good, his actions were illegal."

"But it was so many years ago, and he's gone now. Surely such a minor crime doesn't matter anymore."

"Under normal circumstances, probably not, but if someone with enough influence pressed the matter—"

"Someone like Dr. Walker?"

"Yeah." Damn. Sometimes this job really sucked. "If all this became public knowledge, Walker's reputation won't be the only one to suffer. James Miller will be branded a criminal. What do you think the good citizens of Land's Cross will think of him then?"

"That's horrible." She pushed against his chest, breaking his hold and making him realize he'd been comforting himself as much as her. "You'd destroy the reputation of a wonderful man just to satisfy a malicious, greedy client?"

Her words were like an arrow through his conscience. "We're not trying to destroy anyone's reputation. We're doing our best to circumvent a blackmail threat in a manner that ensures Patty doesn't go to jail and no one's secrets are revealed. In the process, you'll receive a generous settlement."

"I don't care about his money. I was perfectly happy before your client started playing God with my life."

"Walker didn't start this. Patty did."

"And I'm supposed to just go along with Walker's grand plan to fix everything? Just how big an idiot does that man think I am?"

"We never intended to insult your intelligence. Honestly, we merely underestimated your objection to what we viewed as a simple, straightforward transaction. But you have a good point. *I* would never sign anything without a thorough review and shouldn't have expected you to either."

She stopped her pacing and gawked at him. He enjoyed the rare treat of seeing her off guard.

"My apologies for not allowing you the necessary time to review the deal. But fortunately, this weather has rectified that. I checked with the airline this morning and I can't get a flight out until next week, which gives you ample time to consult with an attorney."

Apparently recovered from her shock, she folded her arms across her chest and studied him. Kyle had to fight the urge to scoop her up and kiss her.

"And what if my lawyer agrees that this whole mess is a bunch of B.S. and supports my decision to decline your client's offer?"

"Then I'd recommend you find a different attorney."

"One who sees things your way?"

"No." He deliberately hardened his voice. It was imperative she understand the seriousness of the situation. "One who understands that taking this deal is the only option available if you want to maintain your normal life."

"Is that a threat?"

"No, it's good advice." He softened his tone again. Last thing he needed was for pride or anger to keep her from recognizing his olive branch. "Take advantage of the time, and get a professional in your corner. You're going to need it."

On the counter behind him, the timer dinged, signaling an end to this round—and letting him know the bread was finished rising.

"You can contact your attorney on Monday. You do have an attorney, right?"

"Yes," she snapped.

"Good. I have another copy you can give him to review."

"Aren't you helpful." She plopped back into her chair, wearing a mutinous scowl, like a child who'd been reprimanded for a crime she thought she'd gotten away with. Luckily, he'd gotten a pretty good handle on her in the past twenty-four hours and knew that while she wasn't happy with the situation, she would do what needed to be done.

Kyle bit down on the corner of his lip to keep from grinning as he brushed butter on the dough before squeezing the bread pan into the oven, along with the green beans. When he straightened, he caught his reflection in the microwave glass. A huge flour smear covered his right cheek.

He cut Shayna a glance, and she looked him dead in the eye. Devious woman. The smug expression on her beautiful face dared him to complain, so he refrained from even wiping away the mess.

The flour wasn't the only thing he'd noticed about his appearance. Two days' worth of stubble covered his chin, his cowlick had sprung to life and the borrowed coveralls had stretched out and now hung lifelessly off his body. Time to kick the bargain-box charity-case look.

"We've got about an hour before dinner. If you'll loan me a razor, I'd like to shower and shave."

"Uh, sure. I've got a spare razor upstairs." Shayna stood, a bit thrown by the sudden shift in topic. "Be right back."

Somewhat dazed, she headed upstairs. Was it just her, or did every conversation with that man follow a circular pattern? Why in the world did she ever encourage him to work on his social skills? Though, she had to admit, the way he'd touched her while talking had been nice.

She'd been surprised by the warmth and tenderness of his fingers as they'd wiped away her tears. And when she'd pushed against his chest, she'd been unable to erase the memory of his tight, tanned skin—skin she was dying to see again. To touch and taste and tease.

By the time she made it to her bathroom, her imagination had her heart racing like a virgin who'd just crawled into the backseat for the first time. Who knew she had such a weakness for arrogant, annoying attorneys?

Digging through the drawer next to the sink, she unearthed a spare disposable razor. She wasn't sure what worried her worse—the sexy, clean-shaven Kyle she remembered from California or the sexy, rumpled Kyle who'd been driving her crazy all day. Both were a danger to her peace of mind.

After a quick check of her hair and a refresher on her lipstick, she ducked back into her room.

After all the fights and battles she'd witnessed in the first seven years of her life, she'd never been one for arguments and tense discussions; yet somehow, twice in two days, she'd stood her ground and emphatically disagreed with Kyle. Amazing how good, how freeing, it felt to speak her piece and not back down from her opinions.

Maybe she'd simply been waiting all these years for an issue important enough to make her step out of her comfort zone. Or maybe Kyle's "don't take it personally" attitude provided the safety net she'd always been lacking. Whatever the reason, it was nice to know the world wouldn't end if Shayna Miller asserted herself.

Even so, she was smart enough to realize a couple of vocal exchanges hadn't changed anything. Neither she nor Kyle intended to budge on the issues. She did have to admit, though, calming down and having Chester Warfield— the attorney who'd handled Daddy's will—review Walker's agreement was a smart idea. Not that she planned to cave, but it couldn't hurt to know all her options.

Even though she'd been very young when she'd lived with Patty, she'd never forget the whiplash lifestyle created by her mother's constant moneymaking schemes. The woman had constantly ranted about money, about how being rich was the key to being happy. Of course, even when she managed to get her hands on some cash, Patty was never happy. And neither was Shayna.

Not until she and James had moved to Land's Cross. They'd never had much money, but they'd always been happy. He and Papa Joe had taught her that love and peace, family and friends, were more valuable than money.

How could she allow Walker or Patty or even Kyle to twist the past and paint James Miller as a criminal?

She imagined that at first no one would really care that he hadn't been her natural father, but once the facts became clear, that he'd never legally adopted her, that he wasn't even her stepfather, then things would get murky.

Folks who had known them for nearly twenty years would begin to question everything. All his accomplishments, all the good he'd done for this community, the kids he'd mentored, everything would be overshadowed by the cloud of suspicion.

Amidst all that worry and confusion, would she be able to make people see that he'd been a decent, honorable man all his life, that when most people would have walked away, he stepped up and saved her?

Her heart insisted that, yes, the people who mattered would understand. But her mind was harder to convince.

Chapter Seven

The kitchen smelled like a dream. To honor the scrumptious meal Kyle had created from nothing, Shayna dug out a linen tablecloth and the good dishes, which hadn't seen the light of day in seven years. After arranging two place settings, she added a couple candles and a clutch of black-eyed Susans rescued from the frozen flower beds.

The overall effect was beautiful and festive. And romantic. She nibbled her lower lip. This was not good. The last thing she needed was more temptation.

She scooped her hair out of the danger zone and leaned forward to blow out the candles, but the sound of footsteps in the den froze her lips in midpucker. If she extinguished the flames now, he'd know about her second thoughts. Hating the idea of exposing indecision to such a decisive man, Shayna pinned on what she hoped was a gracious hostess expression.

When he rounded the corner and came into view, her breath lodged in her throat. Man, oh man. He looked as good as dinner smelled.

He was fresh from the shower, with his wet hair looking a few shades darker than normal and combed back from his face. The bump on his forehead was barely noticeable. His jaw looked as smooth as a plump, ripe plum. Yummy.

The coveralls were gone, replaced by the suit she would have bet money had been ruined. The shirt, looking suspiciously as if he'd hunted up her iron and put it to good use, was open at the neck and untucked over his trousers, which appeared an inch or so shorter than the last time she'd seen them. His feet were bare. Goodness, the man even had sexy feet. Too unfair.

Searching for her voice, Shayna ran her tongue over her lips. "Nice." She mimicked his earlier compliment, hoping it pleased him as much as it had pleased her.

"Thanks." He nodded at the festive table. "Looks great."

"After all your hard work, it would have been a sin to eat on paper plates." Thankful her voice and her brain-power had kicked back in, she waved a hand toward the table. "I wasn't sure about the candles, but in this house, real food is cause for celebration."

"I bet." He laughed softly as he squeezed into the kitchen and cracked open the oven. "The bread's done."

As they worked together to get the food on the table, a relaxed, easy camaraderie grew between them. She guessed she wasn't the only one who'd come to dinner determined to put aside their disagreements and enjoy a pleasant evening.

She popped the cork on the wine she had bought to take to Lindy's and poured them each a glass. Kyle held her chair then took the seat adjacent to hers and lifted his glass.

"A toast." He paused while she followed suit. "To good food, good company and no shoptalk."

"Amen," she agreed, clinking her glass gently against his.

For several minutes the conversation stopped as they fixed their plates and savored those first few bites.

"Kyle, this is amazing. Talk about missing your calling."

"I actually considered going to culinary school at one point."

"But you were too hungry for all that money and power, right?"

"Don't forget prestige." He shook his head with a wry smirk. "In my defense, I was only eighteen."

She tapped her fist on the table like a gavel. "Innocent by reason of youth. Nobody should be held accountable for bad decisions made in the first twenty years of life."

"You would have made an excellent lawyer," he teased, popping a bite of ham into his mouth.

"The last thing the world needs is another lawyer. Think I'll stick with social services, despite the lack of power, prestige or money. Besides, the world always needs more social workers."

"Because the work's too hard, and very few people have the strength to go the distance. That's why so many kids fall through the cracks—the way you did."

She wrinkled her nose, hating the fact that he was right. "How come you know so much about the career span of social workers?"

"Back in L.A., I do a bit of pro bono ad litem work, representing kids who find themselves at the mercy of the court. The turnover rate for caseworkers is ridiculous."

Another piece of the Kyle Anderson puzzle, a very appealing piece. Those were some lucky kids, to have Kyle fighting on their side. Good thing he was stubborn and obsessive and representing Steven Walker, or she'd be in real danger of falling for him.

"So why did you choose such a tough field?" he asked.

"Most kids don't get as lucky as I did, and while I can't solve all their problems or single-handedly fix the system, I can make sure that the kids who come to me know someone cares about them. I can show them that they don't have to spend the rest of their lives paying for their parents' mistakes."

"You're truly incredible, Shayna. All that compassion and conviction will make you an amazing role model for the kids you work with. You'll go the distance. I'm sure of it."

Flustered by his kind words, she dropped her roll onto her plate and hid her trembling hands in her lap. "I swear, Kyle, sometimes you're so charming I think you must be part southern."

"It's not charm. It's the truth." His hand tenderly captured hers, his thumb tantalizing her palm. "And for the record, southern men don't have a monopoly on complimenting smart, beautiful, giving women."

Was it possible for bones to actually melt? Sure seemed like hers were. Even knowing it was a bad idea, Shayna couldn't seem to keep her hand from flipping over, her fingers tangling with his. "I think the wine might be going to our heads."

"I'm dead sober and dying to kiss you." His voice was so strong and deep, Shayna felt the words all the way down to her toes.

It seemed to her they'd been building to this moment since his arrival. "Are you having as much trouble as I am remembering why that would be a bad idea?"

Kyle tunneled his free hand into her hair. "I've been fantasizing about feeling your hair draped over my body."

Shayna braced her hand on his knee and leaned toward Kyle's lips. "Any spot in particular?"

"Oh, yeah." His mouth brushed her skin, traveling slowly across her cheek. Her fingers delved into the thick hair at his nape and, tired of denying herself, she turned his head and captured his lips.

The reaction was immediate, explosive. Heavenly.

Kyle quickly took control, his lips exploring hers until he found the perfect fit. Without breaking the kiss, he plucked her out of her chair and set her across his lap, matching her softness against his hardness, letting her feel how much he enjoyed kissing her. She gasped, and he took the kiss even deeper, to a place she thought existed only in love songs.

His right hand skimmed up her thigh, under the hem of her sweater. His skin felt cool against her stomach as his palm eased up to cup her breast, exploring her size and shape. His thumb grazed the tip, and her nipple snapped to attention.

Arching her back, she thrust herself closer to his touch, silently begging for more. He complied immediately, lowering his head and nipping her through her sweater. An excited tingle buzzed through her, ping-ponging between her breasts and her belly.

No longer able to bear not touching him, she set her trembling fingers to work on his shirt buttons. In no time, she had that beautiful, tight, tanned chest exposed.

She grazed her fingertips from his collarbone to his navel. Wanting to taste, she flicked her tongue over a hard brown nipple. He shuddered and released a loud groan of pleasure, which nearly drowned out the ringing telephone.

They both froze. Kyle's whispered curse matched Shayna's thoughts exactly. "I don't suppose you can let it ring?"

"Shouldn't." She shuddered as his teeth nipped her earlobe. "It might be an emergency."

"Okay, but don't forget where we were." He kissed the curl of her ear before pulling back. Shayna stood slowly, not sure her legs would support her weight. The phone's third ring sounded like a trumpet blast.

Her fingers weren't quite steady as she picked up the receiver. "Hello?"

"Well, happy holidays, girlie."

Shayna's aroused sluggishness disappeared in a flash at the sound of Patty's scratchy voice on the line. The phone nearly squeezed through her fisted grip. "What the hell do *you* want?"

Kyle, shirt still unbuttoned and untucked, was at her elbow in a heartbeat, a raised eyebrow silently asking the caller's identity.

"Patty," she whispered. Kyle's face instantly registered the same degree of fury flooding Shayna's system.

"Got company, do you? I'll bet our sexy lawyer friend's a demon in the sheets. Is that how he plans to get you to agree to Steven's silly scheme?"

As her mother's venom poured through the phone and straight into her brain, time spun backward, hurtling Shayna back to that ratty apartment in Boston, where Patty had ruled with an iron fist and Shayna was always too afraid to do anything other than exactly what she was told.

"If he'd offered me a tumble, I damn sure would've taken it. The man's got great hands. You know what they say about a man with big hands, don't you, girlie?"

Suddenly the phone was wrenched from her grip. "Patty, where the hell are you?" Kyle's voice became a background blur as her brain spun.

How could she be so stupid? A home-cooked meal, a handful of sweet compliments, a few steamy glances and she was ready to haul this man—this near-stranger—into her bed, and all this time, he'd just been working his case. If Patty hadn't interrupted when she did, they'd probably already be well on their way to naked and sweaty.

She wiped her clammy forehead with the back of her hand. Kyle's back was to her as he spoke into the phone. "I told you not to make a move until you heard from me."

Were they working together? Disgust rolled through her stomach. Too stunned to even work up a good fight, Shayna left the kitchen. Earlier, she'd sent Brinks outside so they could eat without suffering his begging. Now she stopped at the front door long enough to let him in, then she dragged her leaden body up the stairs.

She should have figured any man who would willingly work for her selfish, greedy birth father would consider sex just another tool to get the job done. Once she and Brinks reached the bedroom, she locked the door, something she'd never done before.

Her movements were jerky as she crossed to the bed, shedding her clothes as she went. She needed to crash. Sleep would keep her mortified tears at bay and give her the strength to work up a good head of steam tomorrow.

She crawled under the covers. Brinks jumped up and settled next to her, one paw resting against her heart. This was the kind of love and support a girl could trust.

First thing in the morning, she was getting that man off her mountain, even if she had to strap him to her back and carry him over that damned bridge. Although, with his bulldog tenacity, she knew getting him back down the mountain wouldn't be as hard as getting him out of her life.

* * *

Kyle nearly lost his train of thought when Shayna stumbled out of the kitchen, her skin so pale that her veins stood out in morbid relief. He wanted to fling the phone against the wall and pull her back into his arms. But Patty was bitching in his ear, threatening to screw Walker by going straight to the media.

This potential danger to his client—to his career— narrowed Kyle's focus back onto the job at hand. "Patty, if you cross Dr. Walker, you won't get one red cent."

She continued to rant and rave for nearly half an hour. He should have hung up long before now, but knowing Patty it would have pissed her off so badly that she'd have acted immediately—the resulting actions harming everyone involved.

Not wanting to see Shayna suffer any more for her mother's mistakes, he talked until both his voice and his vocabulary were exhausted. Eventually she agreed to cool her heels.

The instant he disconnected the call, he raced upstairs to check on Shayna. He never should have touched her. Where the hell was his professionalism? His common sense?

The wine and the candles had gone to his head. Not that he'd been drunk. Far from it. But the atmosphere had lulled him into forgetting who they were, why he was here. And now he'd hurt her. Damn. She didn't deserve to be used. Not by Walker or Patty and most certainly not by him.

Shayna represented the complete opposite of what he aspired to. Ironic that she was the key to his future success. Of course, if he didn't get a handle on this situation, he would lose everything he'd worked for.

He knocked gently on her bedroom door. "Shayna, are

you okay?" The only sound was Brinks sniffing through the crack at the bottom of the door.

"Shayna?"

"Go away."

"Not until I know you're okay. What did she say to you?"

"Nothing I shouldn't have been able to figure out on my own."

What the hell did that mean? "Shayna, please let me in. We need to talk."

"I think we've said more than enough."

He didn't like the defeat in her voice. Through all the crap that had been thrown at this woman, he'd never once heard her sound weak.

"Go away, Kyle." The light filtering under her door went dark. He stood there several more minutes, encouraging her to speak to him, but eventually he had to concede.

He trudged back downstairs and started cleaning the kitchen.

Both Patty and Shayna insisted Walker had known about the child from the beginning. If that were true, a million dollars was paltry compensation for the abuse of abandoning a child to the hell of life with a witch like Patty Hoyt. Imagine the emotional scars of spending years trapped under that woman's vindictive thumb.

As bad as his own childhood had been, at least the true hell hadn't started until he was ten years old. By the time heroin took control of his mother's life, he'd been big enough to seek shelter when the storms brewed. Had Shayna ever had any protection from Patty?

His eyes were drawn to the portrait over the fireplace. James Miller had been her protection. He'd rescued her from Patty's world, and even though the man had made mistakes along the way—mistakes the world was likely to persecute him for—Kyle knew Miller's actions had been heroic.

And now Kyle had crashed her life, unleashing all that old pain. As a child, Shayna had been resilient enough to bounce back. As an adult, would she be strong enough to recover a second time?

Chapter Eight

First thing Friday morning, Shayna picked her way down the road, sticking to the shoulder, doing her best to avoid the slushy brown patches of ice and dirt. The ground looked as if someone had spilled a giant Coke Icee over the mountain.

Good thing her boots were designed to muck through all sorts of nature's nastiness. It took her thirty minutes to reach Kyle's car. It was nose down in a ditch about two miles from the cabin. The front tires were buried in mud, the hood was crunched and from the way the tires listed in, she figured the front axle was significantly bent.

Stepping carefully into the ditch, she pried open the back driver's-side door and peeked inside, finding nothing except the keys still dangling from the ignition. Bracing a knee on the backseat, she reached in and snagged them. Not that anyone could steal the car. It wasn't going anywhere without a wrecker.

So much for sending him on his way and never hearing from him again. She had no doubt he'd turn rescuing his rental into an excuse to knock on her door and continue pushing Walker's outlandish proposal.

Odd thing was, after last night's debacle, she'd gladly spend hours talking about that ridiculous offer. Even that would be better than discussing how close she'd come to falling for his kiss-now-sign-later game.

After Kyle had finally left her alone last night, she'd tossed and turned until the early-morning hours, trying to come up with a game plan to get rid of him. When she'd finally dragged her groggy body out of bed, she'd bundled up and headed out here to check the bridge, hoping and praying with each step that at the lower elevation, the ice wouldn't be such a nuisance.

No such luck.

Thanks to the steam coming off the water and the freezing wind blowing across the bridge, the road surface wore a thick coat of black ice. The half-mile span was too wide to attempt walking across, except under the most dire of emergencies. And while she wanted Kyle Anderson gone, she didn't want it badly enough to see anyone risk life or limb.

She turned and whistled as Brinks came charging out of the woods, barking like crazy. The past couple of months had been unusually warm and dry, so the dog was loving this cold weather.

Thinking about the lack of recent rainfall sparked another idea in Shayna's head.

It might be possible to cross the gulch on foot, down by Hunter's Pass. Not an easy trek, but if it meant getting Kyle out of her home, she was game.

She'd need a volunteer to pick him up on the other side,

someone she trusted. One person came to mind immediately: Danny Robertson. A widower with two young girls, he was one of the steadiest men she'd ever met.

Of course, he was probably working today. Even in Land's Cross, the day after Thanksgiving was a retail tradition, and as the owner of the biggest feed and seed store in the county, Danny would be hard at it all day. It would be a huge imposition, but at this point, desperation demanded she ask.

The hike back to the cabin took only twenty minutes. Now that she had a plan, she couldn't wait to put it into action. Brinks trotted along beside her, breaking away every now and again to chase a squirrel. By the time they escorted Kyle to Hunter's Pass and returned to the cabin, both she and the dog should sleep like rocks.

Finally. Some good news. If she didn't catch up on her rest before tomorrow night's pageant, she'd be one cranky Ms. Noel.

When she reached the cabin, she noticed the smoke curling out of the chimney and the light shining in the kitchen. The scene stopped her in her tracks. It had been a long time since she'd returned to anything other than an empty home.

She patted her fingers over her heart, missing her daddy more keenly than she had in quite a while. As if sensing her sadness, Brinks dashed over and butted his head against her hip.

"Thanks for the support, boy." She ruffled the hair between his ears, then walked around to the backyard.

The hinge on the porch screen squeaked as she let herself in, pausing to kick out of her nasty rubber boots before entering the mudroom. She hung her overcoat on the hook without breaking stride and continued into the kitchen—

where she came face-to-face with Kyle, brandishing the fireplace poker like a sword.

"Shayna!" His shoulders slumped in relief as he lowered the poker to his side. "Damn it, I thought you were still upstairs asleep."

"Nope." Refusing to notice his cute case of bedhead or the fact that the top three buttons of his dress shirt were undone this morning, she brushed past, tossing him the car key as she went. "I went down to check on your car. It looks totaled."

He caught the key smoothly. "You walked down that ice-covered mountain all by yourself?"

"Brinks went with me."

"The dog doesn't count."

"The dog counts more than most people I can think of." She shot him a glare, then grabbed the phone and began dialing. Her eyes tracked him as he returned the poker to its spot next to the fireplace.

After the third ring, a familiar gravelly voice filled her ear. "Robertson Feed and Seed. Charlie speaking."

"Hey, Charlie. It's Shayna."

"Hey, girl. Heard you got some weather up there."

"Yeah, between the bridge and the sinkhole, I'm penned in. Listen, is Danny there?"

"He's around here somewhere. Hang on a sec, and I'll find him for ya."

"Thanks." She waited several long minutes, concentrating on the sounds of a busy sales day filtering through the phone rather than thinking about Kyle, who had returned to the kitchen and was rattling around behind her.

Finally Danny picked up. "Hey, sweetie, you missed a great spread yesterday. How'd you weather the day?"

"Cold and cranky. You've got no idea how much I wish I'd been able to make it to dinner." She could have avoided her current pickle altogether if she'd been able to stick to her original plans. "I know you're busy today, but I need a favor. A big one."

"Anything for you. You know that." His immediate assurance warmed her heart. They didn't come any better than Danny.

"Can you meet me on the north side of Hunter's Pass?"

"Hunter's Pass? This time of year, the path will be little more than a cow trail. What's going on?" The question was a mixture of worry and suspicion.

"Well, the storm stranded an unexpected visitor up here, and he needs to get off the mountain. As soon as possible."

"Shayna, are you okay? Has this guy—"

"No. No. Nothing like that." Okay, so it was way too much like that, but she didn't see any reason to share her embarrassment with anyone else. "But now that the storm has passed, it would be best if we weren't stuck up here alone any longer. You know how people love to talk."

A warm, creamy cup of coffee appeared at her elbow, startling her. She turned her head and saw Kyle, his expression blank, a cup in both hands.

"Okay, there's obviously more going on here than you can tell me about right now."

She wordlessly accepted the cup Kyle had doctored for her. "That's right."

Danny's breath huffed through the phone line. Shayna could easily picture her abnormally tall friend towering above everyone in the store, raking his hand through his salt-and-pepper hair, his mind sorting and organizing, seeking solutions to problems, looking for a way to answer her plea while still tending to his business.

Guilt started working its way through her pique. She was asking too much. "Listen, don't worry about it. I'm sure the store is really hopping today. Mr. Anderson will just have to cool his heels one more day. The sand truck will have the bridge cleared by tomorrow."

"Nonsense. You obviously need to get rid of this guy, or you wouldn't have called. I can be there by noon. Can you hang in there for a couple more hours?"

"Noon is perfect. Thanks, Danny. You're the best."

Kyle pounced the instant she disconnected the call. "Shayna, talk to me. What's going on?"

"The bridge is still too dangerous to cross today, and your rental's not going anywhere under its own steam. The only other way off the mountain is on foot, so a friend of mine is gonna meet us on the other side of the gulch in a bit. I don't suppose you had hotel reservations, did you?"

"Of course not. I wasn't planning on staying overnight."

"Oh, that's right. You expected me to fall for your charm and blindly sign that paperwork so you could get back to your rich, powerful L.A. life."

She tried to push past him, but he grabbed her arm, stopping her. "Shayna, last night—"

"Last night I let myself forget you were just a pawn in my father's power play, and as a pawn, you simply do whatever you're told. Apparently you were told to get into my pants if that's what it took to secure my cooperation." The faint flush creeping up his face confirmed her suspicions. Gosh, these people were something else.

"But thanks to Patty—" man, didn't *that* sound odd "—I've got my head back on straight. You need to leave, today, and the only way to do that is on foot, so I suggest you bundle up. I'll get you some duct tape to wrap around those fancy shoes of yours. Might be the only chance you have to get out of here without breaking your neck."

She shrugged out of his grip and dug through the kitchen junk drawer, pulling out a roll of gray tape.

"You can't kick me out without giving me a chance to explain."

"That's where you're wrong, Kyle. This is my home, and I can do whatever I damn well please."

"Fine." He snatched the tape from her hands. "I'll go, but this isn't the end of things. Not by a long shot."

Kyle feared his lungs would explode before they reached wherever the hell Shayna was leading him. He wanted to ask her to slow down, but since her legs were a good six inches shorter than his, his pride wouldn't allow it.

They'd been hiking up and down a pig trail at breakneck speed for nearly an hour. After fifteen minutes of trying to get her to talk to him, Kyle had given up and concentrated on not passing out. At home, he spent four days a week in the gym, religiously. He could bench press two-hundred thirty pounds and run an eight-minute mile, but scaling this mountain in a pair of tape-wrapped Italian loafers was kicking his butt.

To top it off, in an effort to stave off hypothermia, he'd piled on his suit, the coveralls, the stained sweatshirt and his wool trench. He felt like the freaking Michelin Man, waddling instead of walking.

Finally, the forest thinned and Shayna stopped. Here, the water was shallow enough to see the pebbles littering the bottom. The gulch was approximately thirty feet wide, and on the other side the mountain looked even steeper.

Brinks charged into the water, but after a few steps, he quickly turned and retreated. "Water can't be more than forty degrees," she said, although not necessarily to him. She hadn't spoken a word to him since before they'd left the cabin.

She took a swig from a canteen then held it out to him. He drank gratefully, trying not to gulp it down like a dying man in a desert.

"The ride back to town shouldn't take more than thirty minutes from here. I called Mrs. Windsor, who runs the Sheltering Arms Bed and Breakfast, and she's got one room available. I told her you'd take it. Danny can drop you off. When you contact a wrecker, make sure you call a local service and tell them your car's in the ditch about a tenth of a mile northeast of the bridge at Shiner's Gulch."

After such a long stretch of silence, her words flew fast and furiously, but when she'd said what she needed to say, she locked her lips and turned her gaze to the far bank.

Now that he finally had her contained, he tried again to apologize. "Shayna, I'm sorry about last night."

"I'll bet you are. If only Patty had waited another half hour or so, you could have finished the job."

"Kissing you had nothing to do with the job. *That's* the reason I'm sorry. Acting on attraction makes business relationships awkward. It's a line I've never crossed before, but with you, I couldn't stop myself."

"Uh-huh. Next thing I know, you'll be promising to respect me in the morning."

Before Kyle could finish his apology, Brinks rushed back to the water's edge and started barking excitedly. He turned to see what had captured the dog's attention, and at first, he thought he was witnessing a Sasquatch impersonator.

Even from a distance, the man coming down the mountain, dressed in jeans and a tan corduroy jacket, looked as big and sturdy as a tree. As he came closer, Kyle estimated him at six and a half feet. A John Deere ball cap covered his head, but his steely brown eyes glared right through Kyle.

The ride back to town promised to be interesting.

Shayna skipped over to stand beside the dog, waiting for the giant to cross the quickly moving stream.

"Danny!" The minute the man touched dry ground, Shayna launched herself at him and disappeared within the circle of his humongous arms. Holy crap. This guy could send professional wrestlers running home to mama.

Kyle watched Shayna's face as she embraced the other man. He had to admit he was relieved to see the connection wasn't romantic.

Eventually Shaq junior put Shayna back on her feet. The minute his arms were empty, Brinks jumped him, the dog's paws extending only to his waistline. His hand stroked the dog as he eyed Kyle, doing a quick sweep. Kyle had to give the man points for not mentioning his absurd outfit. Still, he couldn't help but straighten his spine, as if he could stretch himself a bit closer to the six-foot mark.

"This him?" the man asked, not bothering to disguise his distrust.

"Yes. Danny Robertson, Kyle Anderson." Shayna made the introductions without bothering to look Kyle's way.

Kyle extended his hand, half expecting the behemoth to crush his fingers in a territorial show of strength.

"Hear the weather caught you by surprise." The handshake was firm, and Robertson looked him straight in the eye. They were traits Kyle had always considered indicators of an honest man.

"Sure did. I ended up taking a nosedive into the ditch Wednesday night. Fortunately, Shayna and Brinks were kind enough to take me in." Instinct told Kyle it would be healthier to downplay his attraction to Shayna around Danny Robertson.

"That sounds like our Shayna. Always taking in strays."

Kyle didn't miss the insult but opted to let it pass. It had to be at least twenty miles back to town, and he damn sure didn't want to risk having to walk it. "I appreciate you taking the time to come out and give me a lift back to town."

"Just you?" Danny swung a curious glance back to Shayna. "I figured you'd be coming, too."

"Nope. I'm going home to enjoy the peace and quiet."

"Sure you're going to be able to make it for the pageant tomorrow?"

"The bridge shouldn't be a problem by then, but if push comes to shove, you can drive out here and rescue me."

"Like I said, anything for you, darling."

"I hate to be pushy," Kyle interrupted testily. Seeing her flirting with this man was pissing him off. "But you've got to get back to work and I'm freezing my ass off out here, so I'm ready whenever you are."

Not that he was looking forward to following this guy's mile-long legs up the mountain, but no matter how much his body complained, Kyle would match him stride for stride.

Danny nodded. "Then let's go." He bent and swiped his lips across Shayna's cheek. A flare of jealousy burned through Kyle. Knowing he didn't have the right, he shook off the feeling and followed Danny Robertson through the stream.

His two pairs of pants and five-hundred-dollar shoes were useless against the icy water.

"I'll call you tonight," Danny called out to Shayna.

"Thanks, I really appreciate this." She smiled and waved at Robertson, then headed back into the thick wall of trees and brush without a single glance in Kyle's direction.

Once they'd scaled the steep slope, Kyle was relieved to find a mud-covered pickup parked less than half a mile across a flat, grassy field.

They reached the truck and Robertson quickly fired

up the heater. "I know Shayna's a grown woman and has the right to make whatever choices she wants with her life, but just so you know, if you hurt her, you'll have to deal with me."

He'd expected some form of territory marking, but the country boy's simple, straightforward warning gave him pause.

Crap. Dodging an overprotective, big-brother wannabe would make a difficult situation impossible. Not to mention the roadblock Robertson could represent if he supported Shayna's decision to fight Walker's wishes.

For the sixth time in less that an hour, Shayna paced a circle around her den. She'd insisted Kyle leave, had in fact escorted him off the mountain, and yet, ever since her return from Hunter's Pass, the cabin felt too big, too quiet, too empty.

Unbelievable. The man had spent less than forty-eight hours here. His imprint shouldn't be so strong.

But it was.

She'd found his discarded tie in the spare room. The silk fabric still carried a hint of his wonderful warm leather scent.

She'd turned his leftovers into an awesome sandwich.

She'd had to shut the door to his room so that Brinks would stop wandering in there and whining.

When the phone rang late that afternoon, she pounced on it like a dog after a chew toy. Pathetic. She'd never been so unhappy with her own company.

"Hello?"

"Hey, darling. Did you make it back up the pass in one piece?" Judging by the background noise, Danny was still at work.

"I sure did." She muted the game show she hadn't been paying any attention to. "Thanks again for coming out and picking Kyle up. I know it was a huge inconvenience, especially on such a busy day."

"No problem. Around this place, they're all busy days."

"Did you get him dropped off okay?"

"Safe and sound." Danny had never been much of a talker, but this was ridiculous. Still, she refused to press the subject any further. Sending him back to town had been her idea. Pumping Danny for information like an infatuated teenager would make her look like a fool.

"Well, thanks again. I guess I'll see you tomorrow night."

"You bet. Call if you need any help getting into town."

"Will do," she promised before hanging up.

Sometimes men could be so infuriating. Would it really have been that difficult for Danny to give a more detailed report? Had Kyle talked about why he was in town? Did he mention that smoking-hot kiss and how close he'd come to sweet-talking her into the sack?

"Arghhh!" Her aggravated growl captured Brinks's attention. The dog, who'd been smart enough to nap the day away after all their hiking, popped to his feet and ran to the door. Taking the hint, she yanked her hat and coat off the hook by the door and took the dog out into the moonlit front yard.

She had to assume that Kyle had kept his word and not mentioned his reason for being in town, because if he'd let the truth slip, Danny would've used up a month's supply of words in order to give her the third degree.

Feeling somewhat reassured, she called Brinks back and headed back inside. Before she'd even gotten her coat off, the phone rang again.

"Girlfriend, you've got some explaining to do." Lindy didn't even wait for Shayna's hello. "Omitting facts is practically the same thing as lying."

"I know, but I didn't want to upset you. Knowing you, you'd have hiked up here and chaperoned."

"Are you kidding? It was freezing out there. I'd have sent Travis instead."

Shayna laughed and relaxed into the couch. Gosh, it was great to have such good friends.

"Seriously, though," Lindy said. "What happened up there?"

"The stubborn fool followed me home to discuss the legal agreement Dr. Walker hired him to deliver, then on his way back to town, his car crashed into the ditch. He was banged up a little, and since the icy weather had us trapped, I let him stay in the spare room."

"Did he behave?"

"For the most part. He even cooked Thanksgiving dinner."

"He cooks? Amazing. So why'd you send him packing? Were you tempted to jump his bones?"

Shayna threw her free hand over her eyes. This was the drawback to good friends. Too good at reading between the lines.

"It just got too awkward, being around a stranger 24/7."

"Uh-huh, I bet." Lindy paused, but Shayna bit her tongue. Some things were too private even for the best of friends. The silence stretched for ten or fifteen seconds before Lindy wisely changed the subject. "So what's the deal with Dr. Walker?"

Different subject, yes, but still not something Shayna wanted to discuss tonight. "It's very complicated, too complicated for a phone call. How about I stop by tomorrow before the pageant for leftovers and tell you all about it?"

"Deal," Lindy agreed. "Promise you're okay?"

The love and concern in Lindy's voice nearly choked

Shayna up. Daddy might be gone, but that didn't mean she had no family left.

"I promise." She thumbed off the phone and sat up, staring blindly at the silent television. Actually she was looking forward to talking face-to-face with Lindy and Travis about the can of worms Kyle had opened. Even more than Chester Warfield, Shayna was anxious to hear Travis's take on the situation.

As the oldest son of one of Atlanta's wealthiest families, Travis knew all about the twisted thought processes of the superrich. If anyone could advise her on redirecting Steven Walker's interest elsewhere, it would be Travis.

As for dealing with Kyle "Snake-In-The-Grass" Anderson, she'd have to figure that out for herself.

Chapter Nine

Saturday morning, Kyle kick-started his day with a carb overload in the Sheltering Arms communal dining room, but the boisterous crowd failed to distract him from his thoughts of Shayna and the way she'd dismissed him yesterday.

How the hell had such a simple job gotten so screwed up?

He'd been making progress before Patty's phone call. Okay, so *immediately* before her call, the progress he'd been making hadn't had a damn thing to do with the job, but before that, he had started making headway.

She'd begun opening up, had even shared vital information with him, and despite her lack of trust in him as a lawyer, he was sure she'd begun to like him as a man.

The clatter of dropped silverware broke into his thoughts, derailing him from thoughts of how she felt about him—and responded to him—as a man. He glanced up from his plate, only to encounter frowns from several of his breakfast companions. He inserted a more neutral expression and quickly finished his meal.

She may have waylaid his efforts by kicking him out of her home and refusing to listen to reason, but he still had a job to do. Excusing himself, he went upstairs to retrieve his briefcase.

Dressed in an off-the-rack suit he'd purchased yesterday, he left the boarding house and walked the six blocks into downtown Land's Cross. He'd discovered an Internet café inside the small bookstore downtown, where he could check his e-mail and access the Internet.

He needed to follow up on the information Amanda had sent him Wednesday. Shayna had assured him that forging her duplicate birth certificate was the only illegal thing Miller had ever done, but if Kyle simply took her word for it, he'd be shirking his duty. Regardless of his personal feelings about Steven Walker, the man was his client and deserved Kyle's best effort. That meant following every lead to its conclusion.

He needed to dig a little deeper into Miller's background to see if any other criminal activity popped up. After all, very few law-abiding citizens knew how to locate a forger. His conscience cringed at his mercenary line of thinking. What if his investigation into Shayna's dad uncovered something horrific? Sexual abuse? Drug use? A criminal history?

Confronting information like that about the father she loved would devastate Shayna. Was he willing to completely destroy her in order to satisfy a power-hungry client? To achieve a goal he wasn't sure he still desired?

Of course, if she would simply agree to Walker's terms, then whatever other skeletons James Miller may have would remain hidden.

And he could get off this damned ethical fence he'd

been straddling. His feelings for Shayna made it difficult
to execute his job swiftly and dispassionately. He'd never
close this case and move on with his career if he continued to worry about seeing that wounded look in Shayna's
amber eyes rather than doing whatever it took to accomplish his client's goal.

After ordering a large black coffee and settling into a red-
and-beige striped couch, he fired up his laptop and accessed
his e-mail. Despite the holiday weekend, he had more than
two dozen messages. His clients knew he rarely took time off.

He had work piling up in California, and even though
his partnership hinged on this case, if he ignored his other
clients, he wouldn't deserve the promotion. Partners were
expected to juggle large and small cases. Time to prove he
had what it took to earn a spot on the letterhead.

He fired off about a dozen directives for Amanda to
handle Monday and called a few of his more agitated clients.
Once he'd dealt with all the critical issues, he typed up a
carefully worded report for Roscoe, alerting his boss to the
delay in the case as well as his return to the West Coast.

Correspondence complete, he opened his computer file
on the Walker case and began updating it. He paraphrased
his "interviews" with Shayna, recording the details behind
James Miller's forging of her birth certificate with special
care. Amanda had reported cold, hard facts. It was
Shayna's personal insight that gave the details power. He
wanted to make sure his records were accurate, but at the
same time, he didn't want Walker to be able to use Shayna's
words against her.

After saving and closing the file, he logged in to the
firm's specialized search engine. The database provided
personal, legal and governmental information most people
thought was completely private.

It didn't take him long to confirm Shayna's assurances about James Miller's character. The man was practically a Boy Scout. He'd received a grand total of two parking tickets over the course of his fifty-seven-year life, served jury duty three times and filed his income taxes faithfully.

A quick review of his returns showed that he'd never taken advantage of the child tax credit, so while Shayna's dad apparently didn't mind a little white lie to the school board, he wasn't willing to intentionally defraud the IRS. He'd have to pass that along to Shayna. It couldn't hurt for her to be prepared for whatever legal battles his client might stir up.

Damn it. That was exactly the kind of biased thinking he needed to avoid.

A musical chime from his computer alerted him to a fresh batch of e-mails. Several people had already responded to his earlier messages, but only one was red flagged: Roscoe's. He wasn't surprised that his boss was working on a holiday.

He double clicked it. When does she meet with her attorney? Walker is threatening a trip to Tennessee.

Damn. Considering his daughter's high level of disdain for him, Walker's presence would erase what little progress Kyle had managed to achieve. If Walker showed up now, their win-win would become a lose-lose.

He had to find a way to make sure that didn't happen.

By noon Saturday, Shayna was more stir-crazy than the year she'd been cooped up with the chicken pox for four straight days. She called city hall to check on the sand truck's progress and found out Shiner's Gulch was at least two hours down the list.

Frustrated by the familiar inconvenience, she called Lindy and canceled their lunch plans. If the bridge didn't open before three, she'd be hard-pressed to get herself dressed and ready and delivered to the Knights of Columbus Hall by four-thirty.

Hoping to calm her nerves, she treated herself to a warm soak in the tub before shaving her legs and washing her hair. Now that the time had come, she was suddenly nervous about serving as Ms. Noel. With Walker's request hanging over her head, maybe now wasn't the best time for her to be so visible.

But she couldn't back out. The kids and the community were counting on her. Besides, if she didn't give the festival her best, then Walker won.

Ninety minutes later, she was plucked, coiffed, lotioned, powdered, sprayed and spiffed to within an inch of insanity. Thank goodness she'd never been one of those gals who dressed to the nines every day.

Careful not to upset her fancy hairdo, Shayna slipped into her new red dress. The back zipper gave her a bit of trouble, but once she'd conquered that, she had to admit the costume fit like a dream. Mrs. Hollister, her old home ec teacher, would be proud.

If only they'd learned to make shoes in school. Then perhaps she'd have been able to come up with an alternative to the white, knee-high disco boots Ms. Noel had been sporting for the past four decades.

Cautiously, she approached the mirror in the corner. The woman standing there took Shayna's breath away. Between the tousled hairdo and the snug red dress, she actually looked...sexy. In a "Secret Nightlife of Small Town Librarians" kind of way.

The new costume flattered her hourglass figure without

making her look like a harlot, and the faux fur that outlined the scooped neck, cuffs and A-line skirt gave the garment a sophisticated yet playful look.

She still thought the boots were ridiculous but paired with the new dress, they actually looked okay. Sexy even. She'd feared they would make her look even shorter, but somehow, the opposite was true.

In the corner, the phone rang, and a niggle of déjà vu raised goose pimples on her arms. She breathed a sigh to see the caller ID showed city hall.

"Hey, Shayna. It's Martha. I just wanted to let you know the bridge is clear. You should be good to go."

She checked the clock. As long as nothing else unexpected popped up, she should make it on time. "Thanks, Martha."

"No problem. Break a leg tonight."

"Way things are going today, I'm afraid I might." Laughing, she hung up and started to gather her things.

Grabbing the bag with her change of clothes, she hot-footed it out the door. As she drove toward the bridge, she was shocked to discover Kyle's car had already been towed away. Boy, he sure didn't waste any time.

Shiner's Gulch bridge still had a few lingering patches of ice clinging to its edges, but she made it across without incident. Just as she pulled into the KC Hall parking lot— thirty minutes ahead of schedule, thank you very much— her cell phone rang. The number was local but not one she recognized.

She cleared her throat and forced a smile into her voice before answering. "Hello?"

"Shayna, thank God. I've been trying to get a hold of you all morning." The frantic voice belonged to Joe Kincaid, whose father had volunteered to play Santa this year.

"Is something wrong with Elmer's costume?" Goodness, after the disaster with her costume, she should have thought to double-check his.

"No, the costume's fine, but—" Joe paused, a tense breath vibrating across the phone line "—Dad's in the hospital."

"Oh, God, Joe. What happened?" She listened as Joe recounted the story of his elderly father slipping on a patch of ice this morning while picking up the paper.

"The good news is nothing's broken, but his back is out. Doc's ordered him to bed."

"Is there anything I can do to help?"

"Not unless you have a cure for orneriness."

"'Fraid not." She snickered softly, glad to know Joe's sense of humor remained intact. "Guess I'm going to need a new Santa, huh?"

"Yep. I'd volunteer, but—"

"Nonsense," she interrupted. "You take care of your dad. I'll find someone else to pose for pictures with the kids."

"I think you're getting the easier end of that bargain."

"I'm not so sure about that."

After finding out Joe had already dropped the Santa costume at the KC hall, Shayna reminded him to call if he needed anything and hung up.

Poor Elmer, she thought, glancing at the car's clock. *Poor me. How in the world am I going to find a replacement volunteer at the last minute?*

Her first thought was Danny, who was always ready to help out, but he was six-six. The red wool pants wouldn't cover a man that tall. Fortunately, the jacket was designed for a "jolly" tummy, so almost any upper body would work.

She considered asking Travis, but he was in charge of the carnival, and that was too important of a job to hand off to a last-minute replacement.

Mentally scrolling through the men in town, Shayna

could think of only three other men who'd fit the suit and would possibly be willing and able to help out at the last minute. As she dug through her center console, looking for a list of committee members and their phone numbers, she saw the duplicate set of documents Kyle had left her.

Kyle. He'd certainly fit the suit, assuming there was enough padding in the state of Tennessee to turn his hard, flat stomach into a "bowl full of jelly." But would he be willing? More importantly, could she bring herself to ask him, considering everything between them?

There *had* to be someone else who could fill Santa's boots. And she would find him. The photo booth was one of the festival's biggest moneymakers.

She headed inside and began her search. A few minutes later, she'd exhausted her short list of right-sized men.

"Darn, darn, darn." She buried her face in her hands. Time to either call the pageant director and let her know there'd be no Santa this year or somehow convince Kyle Anderson to do her a major favor.

Reminding herself it was all for the kids, Shayna snatched up the Santa wig and suit and raced back out to her car. So far, the only bright spot was knowing exactly where to find Kyle. The Sheltering Arms was only three blocks over. So finding her man wouldn't be the big struggle tonight. Convincing him to don a padded belly, a fake beard and an itchy wool costume was the true challenge.

Was it too early for a Christmas miracle?

Kyle stared at the familiar-looking stranger staring back at him in the mirror. The guy had his face, his build, but the wardrobe was a shocker. At least his new clothes fit. And he had to admit, in comparison to the baggy coveralls he'd worn at Shayna's home, the stiff jeans and soft flannel shirt didn't look half-bad.

Laughter drifted up from downstairs where his fellow boarders were enjoying an early supper so they could make it to the Junior Miss Noel Pageant on time. Kyle had declined supper, but he certainly intended to make the pageant.

Shayna might be able to ban him from her home, but she couldn't keep him from attending public events. No matter how badly he'd screwed things up with her, he still had a job to do, and with Walker threatening to intervene, Kyle couldn't afford to waste a second.

After slipping his cell phone and wallet into his pocket, Kyle strode to the door. When he opened it, Shayna stood in the dimly lit hallway, her hand raised to knock.

His heart nearly stopped. He couldn't drag air in or out, couldn't speak, hell, couldn't even think. He'd never seen anything so alluring in all his life.

She looked like the cover model for *Playboy*'s December edition. Wild brown curls cascaded around a flushed face. Kewpie doll lips formed a perfect O. Amber eyes widened with surprise.

The bundle of red material she'd been sewing now covered her body, coating her lush curves like a coat of paint. White fur brushed against her breasts and thighs. Go-go boots sheathed her legs. Kyle had a momentary flash of those boots wrapped around his waist.

All his vital organs flared to life.

"Wow! You look amazing." He felt, and sounded, like a gawky, horny teenager.

"Tonight's my big debut." Her lips curled slightly, but with the tension in her voice, he wouldn't exactly call it a friendly expression.

"So I've heard." Once he felt sure his tongue could

handle compound sentences, he spoke into the awkward silence filling the hall. "I'm surprised to see you here after the way you marched me down that mountain yesterday."

"Yeah, well, you may have caught a lucky break. Mind if I come in for a minute?"

Kyle would take all the luck he could get dealing with this woman. He stepped aside. "Sure."

She didn't even bother to survey her surroundings. "I need a favor."

"A favor? From me? Considering how mad you were yesterday, you must be desperate to ask me for anything." Desperate was good. It gave him the edge.

"You're right. And in this case, you are the last possible candidate I can think of. Trust me, if there were anyone else, I wouldn't be here."

Damn. That stung. "I believe it. So what do you need? A kidney? My heart?"

"No, just your body."

Anytime, any place, he thought, but out loud, he simply said, "Count me in."

"Great." She pulled her hand from behind her back. A large pile of red wool and white fuzz dangled from her fingers. "Hurry and change. We need to be at the KC hall in twenty-one minutes."

She waved the red outfit at him. The white fuzz was a fake beard, and the pointy red hat was unmistakable.

"You want me to dress up as Santa Claus?"

"Yep."

"What happened to the last guy?"

"He slipped on the ice and threw out his back. Please, Kyle. I'm desperate."

"Hold on a sec. It's bad enough I was thinking about going out dressed like Joe Country, but this is ludicrous."

"Don't make me beg. I'm in a tight spot. If I don't get a replacement Santa in the next—" she consulted the bedside clock "—nineteen minutes, the festival will lose tons of revenue and the kids will be horribly disappointed."

"How does Santa bring in revenue?"

"Every year, the festival has a photo booth where parents make a donation in exchange for having their kids' pictures taken with Santa. They use their own cameras, and most parents send the pictures out as Christmas cards."

It was a great concept. Families got affordable snap-shots, and the community raised money and fostered the Christmas spirit.

"This is important, Kyle," she insisted. "The money goes to buy Christmas presents for our local foster kids, and no one else can do it at the last minute like this."

"What about your buddy Danny?"

"He doesn't fit the costume. Plus, his youngest daughter is competing in the pageant. He needs to be backstage with Tina." She didn't fidget and her eyes remained steady on his, but he couldn't help noticing the slight tremor in her fingers. "Please. I really need your help."

She sucked her lower lip between her teeth, and he realized she expected him to say no. Lord knew, any ratio-nal man would, but the weird thing was, he didn't want to be just another person who'd disappointed her. How she'd managed to work her way around his normal boundaries he didn't know, and honestly, at the moment, he didn't care. Right now, tonight, helping her, finding a way to put the smile back on her face became his number one priority.

"Okay. I'll do it." He took the costume from her limp fingers. Actually, after the stress of the past couple of days, playing Santa sounded like a blast. Growing up in and out of foster care himself, he'd developed a natural ease with kids, but lately, he'd been so focused on his career, it had been years since he'd been around anyone under the age of eighteen.

"You will?" The stunned look on her face was priceless. "Really? Just like that? No strings attached?" Obviously, she'd expected him to make her really beg, or worse yet, take advantage of the situation. And honestly, either scenario would have been a better career move, but at the moment, advancing his career took a backseat to raising money for needy kids—and making Shayna happy.

"Sure. Like you said, it's important." Since his room didn't have a bathroom, he tossed the costume on the bed and started unbuttoning his shirt. "Are you going to stay and help me dress, or would you like to wait in the hall?"

The bemused look on her face was the sweetest victory Kyle could remember winning. "Hall," she mumbled as she backpedaled for the door. "Oh." She stuck her head back in, her gaze sliding over his exposed chest before quickly becoming fascinated with the room's rose-patterned rug. "I left the stuffing at the hall. And Kyle—" her eyes meet his, her smile turned to full blast "—thanks."

Since the clock was ticking, he changed quickly. The suit hung even looser than the coveralls, but this time, the poor fit didn't bother him in the least. Honestly, this Santa thing actually sounded like fun, and after missing his shift at the soup kitchen Thursday, he felt overdue for a bit of giving back.

Best of all, playing Santa meant Shayna would owe him one, and after the way he'd botched things Thursday night, he needed every advantage he could get.

Several hours later, Shayna finally allowed herself to relax. So far, Kyle seemed to be pulling it off. Amazing.

Getting him to play Santa had taken a lot less arm twisting than Shayna had expected. She'd hoped, deep in the far corner of her heart, that he would step up and help out because it was the decent thing to do. When he did, she'd been unprepared for the joy that tingled through her.

And once he'd agreed, he'd done everything asked of him and done it enthusiastically.

While Kyle was excelling as Santa, Shayna was doing a bang-up job as Ms. Noel. Hostessing the pageant hadn't been nearly as scary as she'd feared. All the girls—and their parents—had behaved themselves. No major melt-downs, no catfights or upset tummies.

Danny's daughter Tina followed in her big sister's foot-steps and won this year's Junior Miss Noel title. Of course, everyone received a trophy and a ribbon. All in all, it was a very successful start to the festival.

Now, with her hostess duties complete, Shayna stood backstage and watched the activity still buzzing around the hall. Several elves, aka the county foster kids, raced through the crowd, expertly avoiding the caseworkers trying to round them up. The Women's Auxiliary League's hot chocolate stand was doing a booming business, as was the Girl Scouts' bake sale.

Someone nudged Shayna's elbow. Startled, she turned to see Lindy's grinning face. "We need to talk." Her friend nodded toward the costumed Kyle.

"I know, but now's not the time or the place."

"You're coming over for brunch tomorrow." It wasn't a question or an invitation. It was a command.

"Yes, ma'am. How are Travis and the carnival doing?"

"I don't know. I was so anxious to talk to you that I haven't even been out there yet."

She bumped her hip against Lindy's. "Go support your husband. I'll see you tomorrow."

As Lindy wandered off, Shayna returned to watching the action. This year's most popular attraction by far was the Santa photo booth. Even though it was after eight, dozens of kids still waited to share their holiday wishes.

All evening, Kyle had sat in the oversized chair, patiently listening to the children's wishes while frazzled parents called out, "Say cheese!" For the ones who needed extra coaxing, he talked and chatted until they relaxed and began enjoying themselves. After each picture, he'd send the kids off with a candy cane and a jolly "Merry Christmas."

Seeing Kyle relate so well to the children had been another of the night's many shocks. She couldn't help but wonder what piece of his puzzle provided that ease.

Shayna acknowledged the stab of jealousy she felt watching a recently divorced mother of two rub her cheek against Kyle's, insisting they pose for a second picture, just to be safe. Not that she had any right—or reason—to be jealous. If one of those women wanted an unethical lawyer who would sleep with a gal for the sake of his career, then they were welcome to him.

Now, if she could trust the glimpses of good she'd seen in him, she might not be so quick to throw him to the hordes.

As the crowd began to thin out, Shayna checked to make sure the hair she'd meticulously arranged to look carelessly tousled was still pinned in place. She wanted to help gather together the "Fostered Elves" as they'd dubbed themselves, and make sure they all got their pictures taken with jolly young St. Nick.

She spied Tommy Hunter, looking like a truly mischievous elf, tucked behind a giant Christmas tree. Even though he was only eight, Tommy was a born leader. Once he was corralled, the other kids would be much easier to round up.

Tiptoeing as quietly as she could in her clunky white boots, Shayna snuck up behind the skinny boy and tapped him on the shoulder. "Excuse me, sir," she whispered. "I'm looking for the elf king. Do you know where he is?"

A round face poked out from between the branches. His front teeth were missing, ragged brown bangs hung over his forehead and several large freckles covered his nose. He smelled like little boy sweat and hot chocolate.

Tommy pointed toward Kyle and the dwindling line of photo-seekers. "The elf king sits over yonder, fair lady."

She shook her head and grasped his sticky hand. "That one's an imposter. I believe you are the real elf king, my lord."

She tugged and Tommy came without protest. "You've discovered my secret, lassie." He laughed, adopting a leprechaun brogue. "Guess you'll be wantin' me gold."

What she wanted was a hug but knew it would embarrass him. "No gold, sire. 'Tis a photo I be wanting."

Together, they took their place at the end of the line. As predicted, the other children soon stood clustered around them, curious to see what fun and excitement Tommy was stirring up.

When they finally reached the front of the line, Santa's sparkling blue eyes hit her with a hot look she prayed the children were all too young to understand. Her nerves fired to roaring, ecstatic life.

After smoothing her damp palms over her hips, she waved Tommy toward Kyle's lap, but the boy stepped aside and let the little girl standing behind him go ahead. As Shayna stood in the proud parents spot taking pictures of the kiddos, Tommy, the self-appointed big brother, made sure all the others got a turn.

There were no requests for bikes or dolls from this group. Some of the under-fivers asked for a new family, but mostly the kids mugged for the camera, refusing to tell "Santa" what they wanted for Christmas. These kids had stopped believing in magic years ago. If not for James Miller, she would have become just as jaded and hardened as these kids.

By the time Tommy's turn came around, Shayna was fighting back tears. She, too, wanted all these kids to get new families for Christmas, but that wasn't possible. For now, she'd have to settle for giving them the simple, *normal* memory of sitting on Santa's lap.

Mustering a happy smile, she gestured to Tommy. "Climb on up, my lord. I want a shot of the two elf kings."

He wrinkled his freckled nose. "No thanks, Miz Shayna. Santa's for babies."

A call from the children's caseworkers saved Shayna from making a response, not that she could've. Her heart broke further as she listened to the group singing "We Wish You a Merry Christmas" as they made their exit.

With the last note still ringing in the nearly empty room, Shayna sniffed back her tears and headed over to thank Kyle for service above and beyond the call of duty. As she approached the oversized thronelike chair, she noticed Jolene Murdoch bearing down on them.

"Oh my! Don't you two make a darling couple. I must get a picture for the paper." Jolene, a recent addition to their community, managed the twice-weekly Land's Cross Gazette, and as far as Shayna could tell, the tall, energetic redhead ran the paper single-handedly.

"Jolene, you've already taken dozens of pictures of me with the contestants. How about if I e-mail you a photo of one of the county kids sitting on Kyle's lap?"

"Kids on Santa's lap? That's been done to death." She shook her head. "A couple of young, attractive holiday icons? That's news!" She chuckled and waved her hand, motioning Shayna onto Kyle's lap. "Climb on up."

The idea of plunking herself across Kyle's thighs like the dozens of foolish women she'd watched earlier held no appeal. "I'm sure Kyle's too tired to pose for any more pictures." She hoped he'd play along with the excuse, but when his brows wiggled conspiratorially, she knew he intended to make her suffer the embarrassment of a cheese-cake photo.

"Nonsense," he insisted, pulling down his beard and flashing his sexy smile at Jolene. "Any man who turns down the opportunity to have a pretty woman sit in his lap isn't tired. He's dead." His hand struck with the speed of a snake, snapping her into his lap. "I'm most definitely not dead," he whispered against her ear.

During the quick tumble, her skirt flared, settling inde-cently high on her thighs. "You're not dead *yet*," she warned through gritted teeth. Concerned about exposing any more skin, Shayna lifted first one hip then the other, smoothing her skirt more demurely over her legs.

"Will you please settle down?"

"Not until I'm decently covered." She faced him only to find his focus trained below her chin. Following his gaze, she realized her fidgeting had lowered the gown's bodice.

"Okay, look over here and smile!" Jolene called.

"Wait!" Shayna twisted her shoulders away from the camera. "Don't look," she ordered Kyle, reaching between their bodies to pull the fabric back up over her breasts. When she felt properly covered once more, she angled her shoulders forward as she shifted her legs closer together.

Kyle cursed under his breath. The hand at her waist tightened, pulling her body snug against his, pressing her hips into the solid ridge of his arousal. She gasped and froze.

"Ready?" Jolene called. "Smile."

The first flicker from the camera's flash had Shayna's lips curling upward, more from habit than happiness. Kyle's arms wound around her, his fingers settling possessively at her waist. A wave of desire swamped her. She felt the heat sear her cheeks.

As Jolene snapped several more pictures, Shayna did her best to keep a pleasant, G-rated smile on her face, all the while praying that the camera captured only their images and none of the sparks flying between Ms. Noel and Santa.

Chapter Ten

The next morning Shayna arrived for brunch at Lindy's with zero appetite. How could she possibly put food in a stomach still reeling from last night's up close and personal encounter with Kyle?

She could only imagine the facial expressions Jolene Murdoch's camera had captured last night. If she ran one of those pictures in the paper, the gossips would be hard-pressed to believe nothing improper had happened between her and Kyle during their confinement.

Seeing him in that Santa getup and fake beard had turned her on as much as the sight of him wearing nothing but a towel. How twisted was that? For her, last night's sexiness had transcended mere physical attraction. The glimpse inside his personality, the chance to experience the real Kyle, had stirred feelings in her much deeper than mere lust. And that connection scared the bejesus out of her.

Even more distressing, last night, as she'd flopped around restlessly in bed, she'd finally arrived at the conclusion she'd been working toward since Thursday night. She'd overreacted. To the kiss. To Patty's phone call. To everything.

In hindsight, she'd been forced to face facts and admit that she and Kyle had been equally at fault in that incredible kiss. He hadn't been trying to seduce her into changing her mind any more than she'd been trying to get him to forget about Walker's agreement. They'd simply been two healthy adults caught up in a wild, mutual attraction. The setting and proximity had overwhelmed both their good intentions.

Not that she was in any way excusing their behavior. Any kind of intimacy between them was a very bad idea. As fabulous as kissing Kyle had been, it couldn't happen again. While she no longer thought of him as one of the bad guys, he did represent them. That made him off-limits by association.

She grabbed the envelope holding Walker's agreement and stepped out of her car. Rufus, Lindy's ancient bloodhound, waddled out from under the front porch and howled once, but they both knew it was just for show. After lavishing some love on the old dog, she scaled the porch, and with a single knock of announcement, she let herself in.

"Good morning, gang."

"Morning, Shayna. In the kitchen."

As comfortable here as she was in her own home, Shayna strolled down the long hallway to the back of the house. The mouthwatering smells of coffee and bacon greeted her. Okay, so maybe she could stomach a bite. Or two.

"Where's that good-looking husband of yours?" she asked Lindy as she kissed her cheek.

"I sent him out to gather fresh eggs."

"Amazing how well you've managed to train that city boy."

"Hey," Travis called out from the mudroom. "I heard that."

"Did I lie?" Shayna challenged him.

"Nope. I just wanted to make sure you girls knew I was here so you wouldn't talk about me in front of my back." Travis deposited the fresh eggs in the sink and stole a kiss from his wife, who was busy rolling out biscuits.

Who would have thought two years ago, when a secret provision in Lindy's grandfather's will had forced these two to work on their troubled marriage, that they'd ever be this blissfully—and enviably—happy?

After popping her biscuits in the oven, Lindy wagged a motherly finger in Shayna's face. "Enough stalling. Tell us what's going on."

Assuming that Lindy—who knew all there was to know about Shayna's background—had already brought Travis up to speed, Shayna jumped right in. "Dr. Walker intends to counter Patty's blackmail threats by going public with my existence. He's offering me a million-dollar settlement in exchange for appearing on his talk show so he can play father of the year and compensate me for all my years of poverty and suffering."

"'Poverty and suffering'? That's the most ridiculous thing I've ever heard."

"Oh, wait. It gets better. In exchange for his compensation, I have to support his bogus claim that he never knew about me and promise to never say anything negative about him, publicly or privately."

"Are you saying he's known about you all along?" Travis asked.

"According to Patty, Walker's talk about having recently

learned about me is total fiction. She swears he knew, from the very beginning. And now that she's threatened to tell the world, he suddenly wants to recognize my existence and 'make amends'? I don't think so."

"Do you have any legal proof that he's known about you all along?"

"What would it matter?" Her hands started twirling through the tail of her braid. "Digging up proof and fighting his claim would just drag this out, and I certainly don't want that. I just want them all to leave me—and Daddy— out of this."

"What does James have to do with this?"

"If I go on national television and make nice with that jerk, it will stir up lots questions, and I don't have good *legal* answers for all of them. I'm afraid that when the story gets out, people will persecute Daddy for the decisions that saved my life and made us a family." How could she possibly betray his love and loyalty by casting suspicions on his actions, by going back on her vow to be his daughter for the rest of her life?

"Shayna," Travis said gently, leaning forward in his chair. "I won't deny that when people first learn the *facts* about your history, James might initially come off looking bad. *But,*" he stressed as she attempted to interrupt, "those same facts, along with his impeccable reputation, will also exonerate him."

She exhaled in relief. That had been her hope, but hearing a man with Travis's experience say the words calmed her lingering fears.

"However," Travis continued cautiously, not allowing her time to savor his consensus. "You have to know that if you don't cooperate, Walker will likely escalate this issue until every piece of your life has been made public.

A man in his position doesn't take defeat or disobedience well."

"Kyle implied that Walker wouldn't react kindly if I refused his offer. He said the legal agreement was designed to be a win-win compromise and my only good shot of putting this behind me with any kind of speed and moving on with life."

"I'm inclined to agree." Travis hefted the legal documents. "This looks like the closest you'll come to a victory."

"How? The only winners I see are Walker, who gets to keep his sterling reputation, and Kyle, who earns his partnership. What do I get?" Her shoulders slumped under the weight of her worries.

"A million dollars?"

She shook her head, pulling her hair free from her nervous fingers. "I can get by fine without his guilt money."

"But with it you can do so much better than merely get by."

She sat up and stared into his baffled expression. Guess it was difficult for someone with Travis's background to understand why anyone would choose to live without gobs of money.

"Whether he knew about me all along or not, Walker sees my birth as a huge mistake he can fix by throwing money at me. If I take *anything* from him, he wins. It'll be like agreeing that my existence is meaningless."

Lindy cupped her hands over Shayna's. "Sweetie, you're giving that man way too much credit. He can't change who you are or belittle your life unless you allow it."

"Lindy's right." Travis seconded his wife's opinion. "I never had the pleasure of meeting your dad, Shayna, but from everything I've heard, seeing you so eaten up with ugly, negative feelings would have broken his heart."

Shayna's shoulders straightened slightly. "He never

believed in holding grudges. He used to tell me all the time that hatred could destroy a person's soul and that if you kept it inside long enough, it would poison you."

"He was big on forgive and forget, wasn't he?" Lindy remembered softly.

Shayna sighed. "Yeah, but some wrongs are too cruel to be forgiven."

Late Sunday afternoon, Kyle walked the half mile separating the boarding house from the giant discount store that was hosting the Noel Festival Toy Drive. A large white tent had been erected in the parking lot. Shayna, looking as scrumptious as she had last night, stood under the awning, charming the crowds as Ms. Noel.

Last night, she had jumped out of his lap and disappeared faster than the camera's flash. He'd scoured the nearly deserted hall as well as the dwindling carnival for an hour but hadn't found her. In the end, he'd taken his borrowed costume and returned to the boarding house. If nothing else, it gave him a great excuse to seek her out again.

Turned out he didn't have to wait long. Or look far.

Closer to the tent, he saw a huge load of donated toys had already been loaded up in the back of a shiny red truck parked beneath the tent. A festively decorated table held a metal bucket overflowing with cash donations. He slipped a handful of bills in as he passed.

When Shayna noticed his arrival, she broke away from the couple she'd been chatting with and strolled over. "I was wondering if you were going to put in an appearance."

"Missing me?"

Her skin turned rosy, but she didn't give him a direct answer. "I wanted to thank you for your help last night. You really saved the day. Thanks."

"No problem. In fact, I enjoyed myself."

"I could tell, but I must admit, you don't come across as the kid-friendly type."

Thinking of all the other neglected kids he'd hung out with on the streets, as well as the ones he'd lived with in group homes and foster care, Kyle shrugged. "You're not the only one who drew a raw deal in the parent lottery, Shayna. It can leave a hole you never outgrow. Guess that gives me an edge when it comes to relating to kids."

"Yeah, it helps to understand that childhood isn't all about baseball games and birthday parties, especially when dealing with the kids who are stuck in the system." At the tentative touch of her fingers against the back of his hand, he nearly jumped out of his new boots. He'd never experienced chemistry this intense.

"I also wanted to apologize for overreacting after Patty's phone call and for being so harsh Friday morning."

At the moment, they were alone, but standing in the middle of the Noel Festival Toy Drive. He didn't figure that would last. Cupping her elbow, he steered her to the tent's far corner. "Shayna, I don't know what your mother said to you, but I swear I never laid a hand on her."

"Don't worry. I've never thought you were scuzzy enough to be involved with Patty."

The humorous twinkle in her eyes lifted a weight from Kyle's shoulders. He couldn't stomach the idea of Shayna thinking he'd be interested in someone as false and manipulative as Patty Hoyt. "And for the record, kissing you had nothing to do with my job."

"I know that. Now." Her fingers tapped her shoulder, but not finding her braid there to toy with, she dropped her hand and worried the fur at her wrist. "The truth is, I freaked out. I'm powerfully attracted to you, Kyle, and I'm not happy about it. I tried very hard to ignore my feelings. When that didn't work, I blamed you and that wasn't fair. I'm sorry."

"You weren't the only one who lost control."

"I noticed." Her low, sultry laugh hit him below the belt.

Before he could respond, a mother and daughter called Shayna's name from across the tent, reminding them of their public exposure. She moved back toward the red truck and returned the mother's wave.

Ready for a safer topic, Kyle followed her and gestured toward the clusters of people donating cash and toys. "Impressive turnout. I wouldn't have guessed there were this many people living in a town as small as Land's Cross."

She smiled cheekily in response to his obvious subject change. "Not all these folks live in town. In a big city, if you travel twenty miles to visit a particular shop or restaurant, you're likely to pass dozens of similar businesses on the way. Around here, people drive twenty or thirty miles to get to Land's Cross because it's the only option."

"A monopoly, of sorts."

"Ooh, I love that game." Shayna looked over her shoulder, where a scrawny boy in need of a haircut sat in the truck bed, sorting through the donated toys. Kyle recognized him from last night as the little boy who'd refused to sit in his or, rather, Santa's lap. "Tommy, add Monopoly to the wish list."

"Miz Shayna, how do you spell it?"

A pack of elderly ladies approached the table before she could answer. "I'll help him," Kyle volunteered.

"Are you sure? It can wait, if you've got something else you need to be doing."

"Nope. The only thing on my agenda between now and my return flight Tuesday afternoon is waiting for you to speak with your attorney."

"Ahh, so you've been forced to take a vacation."

"Guess so." He scowled at the idea. He was a man with a plan. He didn't have time for a vacation.

"Poor baby," she purred. "Don't worry. I'm sure you'll survive. In fact, you might accidentally enjoy yourself." Shayna chuckled and patted his bicep. Even that brief friendly gesture snapped his desire to life. Enjoying himself—naked, with her—was exactly what he feared if he had to spend time in Land's Cross without the barrier of his job.

He had to stick his hands in his pocket to keep from grabbing and kissing her. "Accidents do happen." Aware of all the people watching them, he forced a lazy grin. "I'll go help the kid."

"Thanks," she whispered as he passed, then raised her voice in greeting. "Hello, ladies. You look lovely this afternoon."

Her lilting voice faded as he approached the truck. Seasoned brown eyes in a freckled face looked him over, sizing him up. When the kid raised his pencil over the legal pad in his lap, Kyle figured he'd passed muster.

As Kyle began slowly calling out the proper spelling, he noticed scraps of the same yellow paper taped to the boxed toys. Each piece held a different name, all written in the same scratchy lettering. Not a single package was tagged "Tommy."

"Lotta good loot here."

The boy looked up, squinting from beneath the shaggy hair coating his forehead. "You're that fake Santa from last night," he accused. "I don't believe in Santa Claus."

"You don't?"

"Nope." Arms crossed over his chest, the boy wore a battle-ready look Kyle remembered well from his own childhood.

Somewhere, a portable stereo played Christmas carols. As Kyle stared into the boy's world-weary expression, "Little Drummer Boy" faded into "Joy to the World," and another memory, a rare, happy recollection, surfaced in his brain, providing him with a rebuttal to Tommy's skepticism.

"Ever hear the legend of St. Nicholas?"

Tommy shook his head no. Kyle levered himself onto the lowered tailgate and waited, hoping the child's curiosity would draw him to Kyle's side. Sure enough, a few seconds later, the boy dropped down next to him, his feet dangling about a foot higher than Kyle's.

"Hundreds of years ago, this rich guy named Nicholas went to work for the church. During his travels, he met lots of people—mostly sailors and children—who needed help. So Nick used his wealth to buy food, clothes and toys for these people."

He glanced at his audience from the corner of his eye. The boy sat with his head tilted, his attention rapt. Satisfied to have pierced the kid's tough-guy act, Kyle continued.

"Before long, St. Nick's generosity became legendary. To this day, people exchange gifts to honor his memory. We've turned the legend of St. Nicholas into Santa Claus, making him a symbol of the holiday spirit."

"Cool story, but Santa's still just some made up dude in a funny suit."

"You sure about that?"

"Yeah."

"Okay." Kyle nodded, as though swayed by Tommy's answer. They sat side by side for a minute, legs swinging. "So, what's the deal with all the name tags?"

He sensed more than saw Tommy's shoulder lift in a don't-know-why-I-bother shrug. "Making sure the little ones get what they want."

"Cool," he mimicked the boy's earlier bored tone. "Know what that makes you?"

"What?"

"Santa Claus."

"No way, man. That's stupid."

"Think about it. The world's population is a couple of billion, right?"

"So?"

"So, it's not possible for one person to distribute gifts to all those people. That's why the real St. Nick isn't just one man or woman or even one kid. Santa Claus is really hundreds—heck thousands, hundreds of thousands—of people, all working together to deliver the Christmas spirit."

Tommy stared into the distance. Kyle could practically hear the cogs whirring in the kid's brain. "So all the people who brought this stuff are Santas, too."

"That's the way I figure it."

Dirt-colored hair rustled against the boy's collar as he nodded his head. "That's a good story, Mr.—"

"Anderson, but you can call me Kyle." He extended his hand, and even though he knew the answer, he asked, "What's yours?"

"Tommy. Tommy Hunter." He slipped his small hand into Kyle's and squeezed firmly.

"Pleasure to meet you, Tommy Hunter."

The clang of church bells overlapped Kyle's words. Tommy sprang to his feet, tucked the notepad under a pile of jigsaw puzzles and jumped to the ground.

"I gotta go, Mr. Kyle. We're supposed to meet back at the bus at five." The boy's wide brown eyes shot over Kyle's shoulder, his smile growing to show the hole where his left incisor used to be. "Bye, Miz Shayna. See you next week!" Waving frantically, the boy raced off.

Kyle craned his head over his shoulder. Shayna stood a few feet away, wearing that outrageously sexy red dress, her arms hugging her waist. Tears glistened in her golden-brown eyes, assuring him she'd heard a good portion of his talk with little Tommy.

Behind her, the two remaining volunteers counted the cash in the donation bucket. Someone had turned off the music, he realized distractedly as she closed the distance between them.

"That really was a great story, Kyle." Despite her short stature, Shayna easily levered herself onto the tailgate beside him. "Where'd you learn it?"

"A, um, teacher told it one year, when some of the kids started spreading rumors that Santa wasn't real."

"How old were you?"

"About Tommy's age, I guess. Eight. Maybe nine."

"You see something of yourself in him."

"Yeah. A little."

The ladies at the table finished tallying the donations and called their goodbyes. Shayna waved back. The movement stirred her appealing vanilla scent. His mouth watered.

God, could this woman get any further under his skin?

To keep from reaching for her, from stretching her out in the back of this truck and finding out just how far *into* her skin he could get, he clutched the edge of the tailgate and stared straight ahead. All around them, the town was rolling up the streets and turning in, the quiet of the early evening a welcome contrast to the afternoon's commotion.

His fingers began to cramp, but he didn't release his grip on the tailgate. Maintaining his distance, keeping his cool, was crucial. If he crossed that line and touched her again, he wouldn't be satisfied with a kiss.

"Actually, he reminds me of this kid who lived in the

home—our home—for a few months. Curtis Devon. Curt was a scrapper, always ready, willing and able to throw the first punch."

"That does sound like Tommy. Did you two get into trouble together?"

"No. Curt was a couple years younger than me. I usually ended up hauling him to the house after some bigger kids had kicked his butt."

"What did your folks say about that?"

"My folks? Oh, I ah, wasn't living at home at the time."

Shayna's brow rose, but thankfully, she didn't pursue the whereabouts of his parents. "So what happened to Curt?"

"One night his dad got more drunk than usual and broke Curt's nose and a couple ribs."

"Poor baby. Was he okay?"

"Eventually." Kyle's fingers released the tailgate and furled into fists at his sides. Even after all these years, the memory still sparked a vicious anger. "That was the last time the old man ever laid a hand on his son again. I talked Curt's caseworker into pressing charges. I even testified. The SOB got eight years."

"I'll bet that's the real reason you became a lawyer. Sounds like the system worked that time and you must have been impressed by the lawyer who helped Curt escape his father."

It was a damn fine theory, one Kyle had considered himself a time or two, not that he intended to tell her. She saw through him too easily as it was.

"Nah. It was the money." He lightened his tone, hoping to steer the conversation to more comfortable ground. But Shayna apparently had other plans.

She put her hand on his knee and squeezed reassuringly. The electric spark, always there whenever they touched, hummed as an undercurrent to a powerful sense of support and kindness. "So, how long were you in the system?"

He should have known she'd piece together the truth he was trying to keep hidden.

She asked the question so softly, her words sounded like a natural element of sundown, as expected as the stars, so natural in fact, he never considered not answering her.

"My mom was a junkie, and my dad was a two-bit criminal. I was bounced in and out of foster homes for about ten years. Till I turned fifteen."

"Fifteen? That's awfully old for an adoption."

"I wasn't adopted. After the convenience-store thing, I finally realized that if I didn't get away, I would end up like my old man, stealing cars and dealing. I started searching for a way out and learned about a scholarship to an exclusive boy's school. I don't look back."

"We all look back. It's only natural." A crisp breeze blew across the darkening parking lot. Shayna shivered, her shoulder brushing his. Without conscious thought, he threw his arm around her and pulled her in close to his side.

"I saw you stick a wad of cash in the donation bucket," she said softly against his chest. "Thanks."

"Like you said, it's important."

After a couple minutes of pleasant silence, Shayna pulled away and turned, sitting sideways on the tailgate, her knee folded against the side of his thigh.

"I talked with a friend of mine today about the paperwork you brought. He…gave me quite a bit to think about. He agreed with you about talking with a lawyer before doing or saying anything I'd regret."

"Smart friend."

"Yeah, but I can't help wishing he had agreed with me that it's all a pile of malarkey, and I have every right to be pissed."

"No one said you can't be angry, Shayna. But you've got to find a way to work around your emotions and make logical decisions."

"Yeah. Travis said that, too."

Travis, husband to pregnant friend Lindy. Kyle had met them both at the ground breaking and again last night. Neither had bothered to hide their suspicions. Or their support for Shayna.

"Sounds like you've got good people in your court."

"I do, and speaking of which, I've gotta get Travis's truck unloaded and back to him so I can get home and check on Brinks."

"I imagine that monster's got a nasty way of showing his displeasure if you leave him alone too long." Kyle slid off the tailgate, amused by the sound of the brads on his new jeans clicking against the truck's steel.

"Darn dog misses you," she complained.

"What can I say? I, too, am good with kids *and* animals." He offered his hand to help her down. He tugged and she jumped, the combination nearly sending them both to their butts.

Kyle widened his stance and stabilized them, bracing his hands around her waist to keep her from upsetting his balance again. Her hands flew forward, palms out, and got wedged between their upper bodies.

A streetlight shone through the white canopy, casting a soft glow beneath the tent. Mere inches separated their lips. Shayna shifted closer, the fingers of one hand slipping between the buttons of his shirt. Her fingertips grazed his chest.

He sucked in a breath as his hands slid down from her waist, cupped her full hips and pulled her body into alignment with his. The fit was exquisite.

She stared up at him, wide-eyed, lips parted. When the tempting tip of her tongue darted out, Kyle knew it was useless to resist. He moved one hand to the back of her neck and tilted her face up fully to his.

"I'm powerfully attracted to you—" he echoed her words from earlier "—and even though the timing sucks, I *am* happy about it." He flexed his hips, grazing his desire against her tummy. "But I don't want to do anything that you're going to regret."

When she grabbed his belt loops and eliminated every whisper of space between them, Kyle's happiness grew even further. Before he could stop himself, he lowered his head and touched his lips to hers.

Chapter Eleven

Oh, wow. Oh, wow. Oh, wow, wow. *Wow!*

Holy cow, did this man know how to kiss. Although, *kiss* was too mild a word to describe what Kyle's mouth was doing to hers.

Assault? Absorption? Heaven?

Whatever you called it, Shayna wanted more.

Obviously, Thanksgiving had only been a sampling of Kyle's talent. Straining onto her tiptoes, she dove deeper into the heady sensations. The firm, warm pressure of his lips, the sexy softness of his skin, the caress of his fingers along her nape.

Kyle's tongue demanded entrance. She eagerly granted him access. This, her mind sang out, was what she'd been waiting for, why no one had ever truly threatened her self-control.

And this was what made him so dangerous. As his lips

and tongue and hands continued to churn her desire to unknown heights, a tiny, barely functioning corner of her brain fretted over this man's effect on her. Not just the physical, although heaven knew that was exquisite. What worried her the most was the way he kept sneaking past her emotional defenses.

When he finally wrenched their lips apart and separated his body from hers, Shayna felt shaky, like a banjo string plucked good and hard and left to sing itself out. She staggered back a step, her backside bumping into the truck. Her breath came in ragged gasps. His did, too.

He closed the gap between them and brushed his lips against her forehead, his arms wrapping securely around her body. "I want so badly to ask you to invite me back up that mountain, but I think we both know that wouldn't be smart."

"Not smart, but certainly fantastic."

Kyle heaved a sigh, his breath whooshing through her hair. "I'm trying to be strong here, and you're not helping."

"That's because you've got me feeling weak." She let her head fall back, causing his lips to skim down her face and settle on her throat. A delicious shiver charged up her spine. "How about one for the road?"

"I thought you'd never ask." His lips reclaimed hers with a gentleness that took Shayna's breath away. This kiss was slower, longer and a hundred times more devastating than the first.

When he finally ended it, he trailed his lips across her cheek to her ear. "I need to stand here just like this for a few minutes before I'll be able to walk without pain. Then, I'll help you off-load this impressive haul."

"Then what?" she asked breathlessly, half hoping, half dreading he'd suggest coming home with her again.

"Then I'm going back to the boarding house to take a cold shower and lie awake all night kicking myself for being such a gentleman."

Kyle had never actually taken a vacation. Dysfunctional families didn't go camping or take trips to Disney World. Scholarship-dependent college kids didn't do spring break in Mexico. Obsessed junior associates didn't indulge in long weekends in Tahoe. He'd never learned how to take it easy.

It was Monday. He should be at the office, working his way up that damned corporate ladder. But he didn't want to return to California until he finished his business with Shayna, and he couldn't finish his business with Shayna until after she consulted her attorney. That could be anywhere from a few hours to forever. So what the hell was he supposed to do with himself until then?

He knew what he wanted to do. What he'd nearly done last night.

Unable to stomach another huge, drawn-out breakfast with his festive housemates, Kyle dressed in his new suit, slipped out the back door and headed for the local diner. Images of Shayna had haunted and taunted him all night, and now, his exhausted body and brain craved large amounts of thick, strong coffee.

What the hell had prompted last night's uncharacteristic show of chivalry? He'd had a warm, willing woman in his arms, a woman he'd been craving, and rather than pursue her blatant eagerness, he'd planted a chaste kiss on her forehead and hauled his stiff body to bed. Alone.

It was the right thing to do, he knew, but it damned sure hadn't been easy. No matter how much he desired her, he had to stay away from her. Bible-belt girls like Shayna grew up dreaming about happily every after. White weddings and picket fences. Kids and puppies. That kind of heartfelt commitment wasn't in the cards for him.

It didn't take him long to reach the diner, yet at least a dozen people acknowledged him. The way these people made pleasant and friendly contact with a stranger on the street unnerved him. In Los Angeles, if you were forced to cover any distance on foot, you damned sure didn't voluntarily draw the attention of other pedestrians. God only knew who would try to talk to you or accost you.

The diner was loud and crowded, but he lucked into an empty booth by the large plateglass window. He grabbed a seat and ordered a pot of coffee from a passing pink-uniformed waitress. A check of his watch showed 8:47 a.m. He cringed. Normally, he'd be three hours into his workday by now.

"Morning, Santa."

Surprised by the friendly greeting, Kyle looked up. Way up. Danny Robertson, holding a tray of steaming mugs, smiled down. "Good morning," Kyle answered carefully, waving a hand toward the empty seat across from him. Danny had been cautiously friendly after his initial warning Friday morning, but if he'd found out about Kyle and Shayna's public make-out last night, things could get ugly.

Robertson leaned his hip against the vinyl booth seat, gesturing with the tray of hot coffee. "I can't stay. Just wanted to say thanks for stepping in Saturday. You did every parent in town a huge favor. If Santa hadn't shown up, we would have to dress our little angels—again—and take 'em to the mall." He shivered dramatically. "I hate the mall."

Assured his visitor didn't intend to take a swing at him, Kyle grunted humorously. As he recalled, Robertson had escorted two small girls to visit Santa, "Well, with daughters, you don't stand a chance in hell of avoiding it."

"Don't I know it." He jostled the tray, resting it on one leg. "You plan on reprising your role for the parade this Saturday?"

The parade gig came as a complete surprise. "I haven't been asked."

Robertson jerked a shoulder. "Shayna's probably waiting to see if Elmer's back heals. She'd hate to insult him by assuming he wouldn't be up to the task."

"Probably so," Kyle agreed, not believing the excuse for a second. More likely, she wanted Kyle gone badly enough to resume her Santa search from scratch.

Danny stood and extended his free hand. "Well, thanks again, man."

Kyle accepted the handshake. "No problem."

Robertson left and the waitress, Millie according to her name badge, returned, carrying his coffee and a newspaper tucked under her one arm. "What can I get 'cha, hon?" Millie asked absently, her gaze focused out the big glass window.

All he really wanted was the coffee, but since he didn't have anything else to do, he ordered blueberry pancakes and a large glass of milk.

"Anything else?" Millie asked, finally dragging her eyes back inside. "Oh, hey! You're the guy from the paper." She unfolded the paper she carried and opened it to the front page. "See?"

He focused on the five-by-seven full color photo of himself and Shayna. She looked incredibly sexy. He, on the other hand, looked tortured. Just remembering the feel of her in his lap had him tightening. She'd rubbed all those supple curves against him until he'd been highly unfit to be in a room full of kids.

"Yep, that's me. Can I keep this?"

"Sure thing, hon." A bell dinged on the counter, and Millie excused herself. Kyle didn't bother looking up from the paper.

The caption under their picture proclaimed, "Holiday Couple Brings New Spark to Festival Traditions." He couldn't help but chuckle. Bet Shayna hated that.

He quickly scanned the attached article and noticed that the reporter was also a big fan of Shayna. She was named as the driving force behind what was being hailed as the most successful pageant in recent history. Proudly, he noted that the Santa photo booth earned a record fourteen hundred dollars.

Wow. He knew he'd listened to a boatload of Christmas wishes, but he'd had no clue that he'd helped to raise so much money for the foster kids.

He took a slurp of coffee before thumbing through the rest of the paper. Bowling scores, birth announcements and school lunch menus. It was a small glimpse into the peaceful, slow-paced life of a small community.

On page four, he finally stumbled across actual news. The road repair at McGuffy's sinkhole was scheduled to begin at the first of next year. Damage from the recent ice storm had closed the skating rink until further notice. The bottom half of the page was dedicated to the youth center ground breaking.

There was an old yearbook picture of Coach Miller, along with a touching and well-written story on his years of service to the school district, highlighting his emphasis on education—he'd also been a history teacher—as well as athletics.

A photo from the ceremony showed Shayna at the podium. The grainy newsprint couldn't hide the glimmer of tears in her eyes or the pride in her smile. She'd looked so spectacular with that green sweater hugging her body, her hair stirring in the breeze.

When he'd first seen her, he'd wondered if the combination of strength and vulnerability had been part of an act, at that point still unsure if she'd been a party to Patty's threats. Those past suspicions sent a wave of greasy self-disgust through his gut. He knew now that Shayna Miller was the antithesis of her scheming mother.

A third photo showed Shayna and a handful of others—among them the mayor and Lindy and Travis Monroe—standing in front of a shiny white ten-passenger van with James Miller Youth Center stenciled across the side. His sixth sense tingled as he read the article. By the time he got to the third paragraph, the veins in his neck were throbbing.

'Reliable transportation is key to several outreach programs we hope to begin instituting immediately,' reported recently appointed Center Director Shayna Miller, who donated the ten-passenger van in her father's name.

The rest of the article disappeared in a blur of disbelief. Holy hell! Did that woman have any money sense at all?

As part of his background work on this case, he'd investigated Shayna's financial situation. It was bleak. She had no retirement plan, only three thousand dollars in her savings account and her monthly income was barely more than his rent. So what the hell was she doing donating a fifty-thousand dollar van to the youth center while her own car looked like it should be pushed off the mountain and put out of its misery?

Coffee and food forgotten, he folded the paper and stood. He tossed a twenty on the table and stalked out of the noisy diner.

Damned woman was living mere inches from the

poverty line. How could she possibly justify spending money she didn't have on a van she didn't even intend to keep for herself?

She was threatening all he'd worked for on sheer stubbornness. He hated the idea of her doing without when a viable solution was well within her grasp.

Walker's money was her birthright. She deserved it. She needed it. And she was damned well going to swallow her pride and accept it.

The quiet of the empty Knights of Columbus Hall helped soothe Shayna's anger at herself, but her frustration still raged. Her lawyer, Chester Warfield, had headed out to the deer camp with his son and two grandsons this morning at first light. His secretary had regretfully informed her he wouldn't be back in town until late Thursday and was scheduled to be in court Friday morning. Shayna begged for, and got, an appointment Friday afternoon.

If she'd called last night like she'd intended, she wouldn't be in such a pickle.

Instead, she'd driven home, navigating more by habit than attention, and spent the night recalling Kyle's beyond-fantastic kisses, lecturing herself about all the sound, logical reasons to be glad he hadn't pressed for an invitation to her bed.

Then of course, all the sensational, emotional reasons why having him in her bed was a terrific idea had surfaced. That line of thinking conjured up all manner of lusty thoughts, which had fueled some impressively erotic dreams.

Not surprisingly, this morning she was a confused ball of hot hormones and mixed emotions. Figuring it best to steer clear of him until she'd made a decision about Walker's agreement, she was holed up, inventorying the donated toys so she could decide how best to spend the cash contributions. Three-thousand four hundred sixty-two dollars and seventeen cents—a new record, helped considerably by the five crisp one-hundred dollar bills found at the bottom of the bucket. Put there by a certain Hollywood lawyer.

Knowing that Kyle was the surprise benefactor only upped his yumminess. If she didn't uncover a few negatives soon, she'd be a goner for sure.

Last night, when she and Kyle had unloaded the truck, she'd been too frazzled by his kisses to worry much about organizing the toys, so the first order of business was to divide the goodies by gender and age. By the time she had everything separated, she'd worked up a light sweat, so she peeled off her jogging suit's zippered jacket. More comfortable in the cooler tank top she wore underneath, she plopped onto the floor, notebook in hand, and began her shopping list.

She'd become so attuned to the building's silence that the unexpected pounding on the rear service door startled her so badly she broke her pencil in half. Alarmed, she raced to the back door. Several strands of hair escaped her clip as she ran.

Heart beating furiously, she turned the lock and wrenched the door open, finding a thunderously mad Kyle Anderson vibrating on the other side. Dressed in a new suit, he looked every inch the spit-and-polished, no-holds-barred lawyer she remembered from the ground breaking ceremony. Had the jeans and flannel guy who'd kissed her last night been a figment?

"Hey! How'd you know I was here?"

"That old heap of yours is pretty hard to miss." He stormed past her.

Wondering what in the world he had caught in his craw,

and knowing he'd tell her soon enough, she shut and relocked the door. "No sense replacing a perfectly good car just because it's seen a few hard years."

"And I'd imagine a new vehicle would set you back a pretty penny. Probably take a single woman without a full-time job quite a while to save that kind of money."

Troubled by his forcefully bland tone, she wrapped her arms across her chest. She'd taken him at his word when he'd promised to back off and give her time to consider her options, but this return to bullying lawyer mode unnerved her. Was he reneging on his promise? Or was something else driving this inquisition?

"Four-wheel drive certainly doesn't come cheap," she answered noncommittally, heading back to the gym, Kyle close on her heels. "But my old wagon's got plenty of good years left in her yet, so I'm not worried."

"With any luck, if it breaks down, the youth center will let you borrow their expensive new van, since you won't be able to afford another new vehicle for at least a decade on your income."

She spun around so quickly that her hair clip dislodged and fell to the ground. Ignoring the wave of hair settling around her shoulders, she propped her hands on her hips and glared up at him. "What do you know about my income?"

"I ran a thorough background check on you, Shayna. I know exactly how dismal your finances are. Damn it, why continue to struggle when you could be living the good life?"

"Who says I'm not living the good life? I have friends who love me, a career I care about, a community that supports me, a beautiful home that's paid for and a dog who thinks I hung the moon. For me, that *is* the good life."

"But you could afford so much more if you took

Walker's deal. You'd never have to worry about money ever again."

Again with the money. He was beginning to sound like a broken record.

"I don't worry about money now."

"That's obvious." He raked his fingers through his hair, knocking the edge off his frighteningly polished look. "If you did, you'd have signed that agreement and snatched up the cash."

"I've already told you that I can't be bought. Walker can keep his guilt money."

"Quit thinking of it as a payoff. It's his responsibility to support and care for any children he brings into his world, and for twenty-five years, Walker has shirked that responsibility. You can't allow him to get away with it any longer."

With sudden crystal clarity, Shayna understood the root of his stubborn insistence. Her irritation gave way to empathy. Kyle Anderson, with all his dazzling charm and brusque confidence, wasn't interested in making *her* father pay for his mistake. Deep down, he was striking out at *his* father.

Instinctually, she yearned to wrap him in her arms and gently share her insight, but that wouldn't work. If she wanted this man to see reason, she'd have to knock it into him.

"What a load of hooey."

As she'd hoped, her childish word choice took some of the steam out of his anger. "Did you just say 'hooey'?"

"Yeah. This doesn't have anything to do with my finances, or the center's new van, or even Walker's ridiculous payoff. You can't punish *your* father so you want me to punish mine."

Instantly, Kyle stiffened. His brilliant, sparkling blue

eyes went dark, obscuring all his inner goodness. "You don't know a damned thing about my father."

"Nothing specific, that's true, but I know enough dead-beats that I could paint an accurate picture. Ruthless, abusive, degrading, cruel. Part-time criminal, full-time jackass."

A dark look clouded Kyle's face. Shayna's nerve threatened to desert her, but she couldn't quit now. He needed to face this truth, and she bet he didn't have anyone else in his life who'd dare force him into it.

"A big, stocky guy," she continued, working hard to keep her voice cool, free of the sympathy she knew Kyle would despise. "A bully who terrorized his son, picked on him for being a late bloomer with a big heart. And poor kid, he probably loved that son of a bitch once upon a time, until it was beaten out of him."

"Stop. Now." His jaw clenched so tight she could see the veins running down his neck.

Praying she'd correctly judged his character and his inherent opposition to violence, she pressed on. "Against the odds, that kid survived with his inner goodness intact, but in order to insulate himself from the past, he vowed to be as different from that horrible beast as possible. His solution—his salvation—became money. Money, power and prestige. Those were the keys to freedom, to safety. To happiness. But it didn't work, did it?"

Tentatively, she reached up and cupped his cheek, her thumb caressing the galloping pulse in his neck. "No matter how much you achieve, you can't shake that scared little boy. Isn't that what you told me?"

The resentment and sorrow that had stiffened Kyle left as quickly as they had come. His body sagged, the weight of his head resting against her palm. Touched by his grief and awed by the fact that he trusted her enough to reveal such vulnerability, she feathered a light kiss over his lips before escorting him to the bleachers. With a gently insistent tug on his hand, she sat them both on the bottom riser.

Giving him a measure of privacy while keeping his hand sandwiched between hers, she focused straight ahead and waited. She could feel the rise and fall of his chest, hear the sounds of his breathing as he struggled to regain control.

When he finally spoke, his voice had a rusty, ragged edge that nearly broke her heart. "I hated him." He didn't look at her, but his fingers tightened against hers. "I used to jump through hoops trying to please him, but nothing ever worked. Eventually, I quit trying. Then he got arrested for grand theft. They gave him two years and processed me into the system. Foster care was ten times worse than living with the old man. Always feeling like a charity case, knowing people only took me in for the money. It made me feel like a thing."

Knowing there was only so much demon-facing a person could handle at once, she decided to deflect the conversation from his past. Besides, she needed to make a point, and she figured Kyle was finally in the right frame of mind to listen.

"Yeah, I remember that part. Before James took me in, I'd done a couple of stints in foster homes where I was just one of a dozen. Some of those people didn't care about the kids, only their monthly payoff from the government."

He inhaled audibly, turning on the bleacher to face her. She could see the realization on his face as her words sunk in. "*That's* why Walker's money bothers you so much, isn't it?"

"Yeah. It's taken me a while to figure out, and now that I have, it seems so obvious. My brain understands your point about my having a right to that money and how much good I can do with it, but my heart just sees it as once more being valued as a commodity rather than a person."

As it always did, talking about the past made her nervous, restless. Her left leg started to jiggle. "I was pretty near the giving-up point myself when James came along. He never cared about money. He sought custody because he loved me and wanted to take care of me, the way he knew Patty never had."

He moved their joined hands to her lap, the pressure of his touch stilling her jerky movements. "You were lucky to have someone like him come along and rescue you."

"He did more than just rescue me. He gave me a real life. He got rid of sad, scared, unloved Shayna Hoyt and created Shayna Miller, a happy, safe, cherished *daughter.* How can I allow anyone to dishonor his memory?"

"That's exactly why you have to accept Walker's deal. It's the only way to make sure Patty won't paint James as a villain."

"I'll admit that part of this deal does tempt me."

He pulled his hand from her grasp and cupped her cheeks, angling her face to his. "You really aren't tempted by the money?" he ask incredulously.

"No. Not for myself. I'm happy with my life as it is. The temptation comes from how much I could help others, but if I accept the money under Walker's conditions—" she squeezed her eyes closed and searched for words that would help him understand "—I'm just not sure I could live with myself if I abandoned my principles and went along with his story."

"You may not have a choice."

She nodded miserably as a tear slid down her cheek. "I know, and that scares me. Agreeing with Walker's story means I'll have to say goodbye to Shayna Miller and become scared, unloved, unwanted Shayna Hoyt again."

Kyle's thumb soothed away the fallen tear. "Shayna, I've met your friends, seen how this entire community adores you. Unloved and unwanted are two things you will never again be."

His kind words, spoken with such warmth and sincerity, brought forth more tears. And a desire to be loved and wanted in a whole new way.

By him.

Chapter Twelve

Sniffling softly, Shayna excused herself and retreated to the ladies' room. Alone in the large gym, Kyle removed his suit coat and laid it over the back of a folding chair. Once again she'd seen through all his bull and found the truth. And this time it was a truth he hadn't even known himself and one he'd been enraged to have pointed out.

Not many men would have stood their ground when his temper was that hot, but Shayna had never flinched. The woman packed a lot of guts and courage and intelligence into one tiny, alluring little package. A package he wanted more than he'd ever wanted anything before—even that damned partnership.

"And hey, for your information," Shayna called boastfully as she reentered the gym, breaking into his wayward thoughts. He was glad to see her tears and sadness were gone. "Just because I'm not driven by money doesn't mean I'm an imbecile. I sold off fifty acres of timber to pay for that van, and if I want to buy another one in a decade, that land will be ready to clear again."

Her spirited laugh tortured him. It was all he could do not to lay her out on the parquet floor and make love to her, here and now. He had to clear the lust out of his throat before he could respond. "I can't tell you how relieved I am to hear you have such a stable savings plan."

The lame joke was punctuated by a chirp from his BlackBerry. Incoming text message.

"So much for your vacation, huh?"

"I'll just ignore it."

"No way. Even if you don't answer it, you'll be thinking about it."

"Must be such a drag, being right all the time."

"Actually, I get quite a kick out of it," she quipped, picking up a notebook full of scribbly notes.

He unclipped the phone and opened Roscoe Thomas's concisely worded message. *Her appointment?*

Tension tightened his jaw. Once again, he'd become so entranced with Shayna that he'd lost track of the job he'd been sent here to do.

"Bad news?" she asked cautiously.

"Reality check. The senior partner wants an update regarding the appointment with your lawyer."

"Oh, I'm afraid it's not good news. I called this morning, but he's out of town. Friday afternoon is the earliest appointment I could get."

He knew the delay should frustrate him, but it didn't. Another sign of how far his priorities had slipped.

He keyed in Friday's date, and once the message was successfully sent, he turned off the phone and slipped it into the pocket of his discarded coat. "Then Dr. Walker will have no choice but to wait a few more days."

"I don't imagine he's going to be very happy about that."

"No, but as his lawyer, it's my duty to make him understand the ramifications of coercing you into an agreement without allowing you ample opportunity to seek the advice of counsel."

"So your vacation is still on, then?"

"Yep."

"You have any fun, exciting plans for the rest of the day?"

"Not a one. In fact, all this free time is driving me crazy."

"Well, if you don't mind physical labor, I could help you kill a few hours."

"Sounds interesting. What do you have in mind?"

"How are your wrapping skills?"

"Nonexistent, but I'm a fast learner."

She cocked her eyebrows at him. "You're quite the straight shooter, aren't ya?"

"Lies tend to lead to apologies. Since I'm not very fond of admitting I'm wrong, I try to avoid it altogether."

"That's a good policy." She moved to one of the six-foot-long tables set up near the stacks of toys. The brightly colored Christmas paper, scissors, ribbons and tape looked like a scene straight out of Santa's workshop. Too bad the G-rated setting couldn't calm his X-rated desires.

"Have a seat. Since you're a beginner, I'll let you start with board games. The boxes are easier to work with than some of the other packaging."

While he sat, she grabbed an armload of boxes and set them near his elbow. Her hair fell forward, tickling his forearms. The scoop neck of her tank top aligned with his mouth. The urge to taste her skin hit him hard. Damn chivalry. Made it impossible for a man to follow his urges.

When she leaned across him to grab a roll of green-and-gold paper, Kyle thought he would explode. Desire throbbed through him, threatening his tightly wound control.

"Did I tell you about the IRS?" he blurted.

"What about them?" She looked baffled by the sudden shift in topic, and who could blame her? Definitely not his smoothest segue, but God knew there was nothing less sexy than the IRS.

"I was doing some additional background work on your dad. It's part of the job," he assured quickly when she shot him a squinty-eyed look. "Anyway, when I was reviewing his tax returns, I discovered that he never took advantage of the child tax credit he would have qualified for as your legal guardian."

"He didn't? That's kind of strange. He was always adamant about civic duty and that kind of stuff."

"The fact that he didn't take the deduction will work in his favor if Walker attempts to defame his character. If you don't still have the hard copies somewhere, I'm sure your lawyer can get them. It's a good idea to have them on hand, just in case."

"Should you be telling me this?"

He shrugged. Sharing his research wasn't particularly a breach of confidence. After all, anyone with access to the database could uncover the same thing he had.

"Okay. I'll pass it along." She rolled her lower lip between her teeth and gnawed on it. Suddenly, the gym felt as intimate and cozy as her cabin. He saw his own desire reflected in her eyes.

This time, she was the one who jumped in with a subject change.

"The toy drive was exceptionally successful this year."

He did his best to follow her lead. "Looks like you

collected enough to give every kid in the county four or five gifts."

"That would be great. And our cash donations were at an all-time high." She stood and grabbed another handful of toys. He couldn't help but admire the way her pants hugged her rear curves.

She turned and caught him staring. "People get very generous around the holidays," he croaked out, trying to keep the conversation alive.

Silence stretched between them, intensifying the intimacy of the situation rather than dispelling it. Finally, she turned her flushed face away and cleared her throat.

"Well, umm, let's get to work, shall we?"

After several hours of hard work and an easy camaraderie that had both shocked and pleased her, Shayna called a halt to the wrapping party. "That's enough. We'll leave the rest to the battalion of blue-haired grandmas."

"Sounds good to me." Kyle stood and stretched his arms to the ceiling. Her mouth watered. His chest looked a mile wide and sturdy enough to hold the world's problems at bay.

Acting on instinct, she stepped forward and ran her palms over his chest and up to his neck. His vivid blue eyes darkened from summer sky to winter rain.

"Thanks for all you've done."

"My pleasure." His arms lowered, settling around her waist with a possessiveness that sent a thrill through her bloodstream. The decision she'd been dancing around all afternoon suddenly became crystal clear.

She traced the pad of her finger over the ridge of his jawbone. Nearly invisible blond stubble tantalized her nerve endings. "Wanna come home with me and have dinner?"

"Do you have any food in the cabin?" he asked, his voice a notch huskier than usual.

"Nope. But we could pick up a pizza or something. Dinner's just an excuse to get you to come back to the cabin with me." She allowed the truth of her hunger to show in her eyes so there'd be no misunderstanding her intention.

The pulse flowing beneath her touch jumped. "Are you sure?"

"One hundred percent." She tried to rise onto her toes and seal the deal with a kiss, but the fingers at her waist flexed, holding her in place. Struggling not to let her disappointment show, she raised her eyebrows in silent question.

"Shayna, I'm leaving tomorrow."

"Will you be coming back?"

"That depends on you."

His words caused her silly little heart to flutter, and in that instant, she knew. Despite her best efforts, she'd fallen in love with this stubborn, generous, secretly kind man she couldn't possibly share a future with. But she could—and would—share tonight with him.

"Me?"

"Yeah. The legal ball's in your court, so the next move will be yours."

Not the sentimental, mushy answer she'd hoped for, but after he left tomorrow, she'd have plenty of time to deal with her disappointment. Until then, she planned to squeeze a lifetime of memories into one night.

She shifted onto her toes, and this time he didn't stop her. "You're not one of those guys who likes pineapple or little fishes on your pizza are you?"

"Would it be a deal breaker if I were?"

"No way. We'd just switch to Chinese take-out."

* * *

The sound of Brinks's barking silenced the nightly serenade of crickets and owls. As Shayna slipped the key into the lock, she smiled over her shoulder at the man about to become her lover. Yum.

For propriety's sake, Kyle had insisted on following her home in his replacement rental, insisting that if he didn't come home, it wouldn't take Mrs. Windsor long to put two and two together. His concern over her reputation was supersexy.

"Careful with that pizza, or Brinks'll snatch it out of your hands."

She pushed open the door, and the dog raced outside only to slide to a comical stop at Kyle's feet. Snout raised, he sniffed the air and pounced on Kyle, who, thanks to the advance warning, held the aromatic box well beyond Brinks's reach. "Down, beast."

Looking completely at ease with her dog, Kyle side-stepped Brinks and let himself into her home. Shayna followed slowly, shedding her overcoat and zippered jacket. She wanted to absorb and memorize every moment of this night. The second he put the pizza box on the kitchen table, she followed her dog's example and pounced. Now that she had him here, she didn't want to waste one precious second.

Ready to feel his skin on hers, she started tugging the buttons of his outer coat free. Once she had them undone, she pushed it off his shoulders, dropping it to the kitchen floor.

She turned her attention to his shirt, but Kyle's hands cupped her cheeks, drawing her focus to his face. "Be sure. Once we start, I'm not sure I'll be able to stop, and I don't want you to regret this."

She looped her hands around his wrists. "No matter what the future holds, I will never regret making love with you."

"But tomorrow—"

She laid a finger on his lips, stopping his words. "Let's just pretend—for tonight—that there is no tomorrow. Deal?"

"Deal." The word turned into a kiss against her fingertip.

Brinks chose that moment to demand reentry. Shayna turned her head, her lips sliding under his hands. She flicked her tongue against his palm then kissed the moist skin. His tremble gave her all the courage any woman could ever need.

"Hide the pizza in the oven. I'll let him in."

"Maybe we should leave him outside. It might be distracting to have him standing at the foot of the bed howling at me."

"Nice to know you're not accustomed to performing in front of an audience." She skipped out of his range as he attempted to swat her fanny. Enjoying the unique experience of lust combined with laughter, Shayna let the dog inside.

Her previous lovers—not that there had been many—had mostly been immature, too desperate to make sure she didn't change her mind to relax and enjoy her company. Another way Kyle Anderson set himself above and beyond the rest.

Unable to control the smile on her face, she shut and locked the front door. When she turned, Kyle was right there, his pupils swollen to huge black pools surrounded by a cool strip of Nordic blue.

Terribly excited by his barely checked passion, she pressed her back to the door and waited.

"Promise me that if I do something you don't like you'll tell me," he demanded gently.

"I don't like all this talking when you could be kissing me."

"Shayna, I'm serious. I'm afraid my control is going to slip, and I don't want to hurt you."

"I'm serious, too. Kiss me, Kyle. It's what I need. What I want."

His lips captured hers with bruising intensity, kissing her until they were both breathless. He released her lips, and her fingers went back to work on his shirt buttons.

The world went dark for a second as Kyle whipped her tank top over her head. Her bra disappeared just as quickly. Cool air brushed against naked skin that seconds ago had been hidden within her clothing's warmth. The sudden temperature change, along with the ecstasy of Kyle's hard hands cupping her bare breasts, set her nerve endings on fire. His thumbs teased her nipples to attention.

"Beautiful." Kyle's reverent whisper made her feel like the sexiest, luckiest woman alive.

She threw herself into his touch, silently begging for more. He answered immediately, kissing the valley he'd formed between her breasts.

"Kyle," she sighed, hitching her legs around his waist. "Please."

His hands cradled her bottom, fully supporting her weight. She flung her arms around his neck and pressed her cheek against his chest. Beneath her ear, the accelerated beat of his heart drummed in time to her own racing pulse.

Kyle started up the stairs, and with each step, the dusting of hair across his chest titillated her bare breasts. By the time he laid her out on her bed, Shayna's whole body was ready to explode.

As if sensing how close she was, he slowed their momentum by taking his time removing the rest of her clothes. When he stood by her bed and peeled his way out of his suit, Shayna thought her heart would stop. She'd already gotten a sneak preview of his beautiful chest, but the entire package was more incredible than anything she'd ever seen.

She rolled to her side and reached for him, easing her hand around his hard silky strength. He swelled even more, his flesh seeming to reach for her.

"Beautiful," she whispered, hoping the compliment would affect him the way it had her.

"It sure is," he agreed. She looked up and found him staring down at her. Her heart filled with the love she knew she couldn't verbalize. Which meant she'd just have to show him how she felt.

She opened her arms to him. He paused long enough to roll on protection then settled himself on top of her, his erection teasing her opening. She strained upward, bringing her mouth to his ear, and all the rest of her body parts in contact with his. "I need you inside me now." She thrust her hips forward, drawing his body into hers.

He froze, his breath and chest heaving. "Damn it, Shayna. I wanted to make this last."

"Too bad. Guess you'll have to try harder next time."

"Vixen." He chuckled in her ear as his body began moving. She did her best to urge him faster, but the stubborn man refused to be hurried. He pumped his hips excruciatingly slow, in, in, in. Slower still, out, out, out.

In and out. In and out, until her blood caught fire. Pulsing waves of pleasure rocked through her, cresting at the spot where their bodies became one. Shayna quit fighting against him. The instant she granted him full control, he sped up. Seconds later, her body ignited. Bright, vivid flashes of ecstasy showered her, as if there were fireworks exploding in her most sensitive places.

She screamed his name, tears leaking from her wide open eyes. With a final, heart-deep thrust, Kyle's body quaked in her arms, and she knew he was feeling the fire-works as well.

Too moved to keep her love locked inside, she traced the words on his back, encircling them in a heart.

You're in deep, Anderson.

Kyle tried to block the dire warning echoing through his conscience. He lay in Shayna's bed, staring out the dark-ened window, his fingers twining around the ends of her hair. He kept his touch light, not wanting to wake her but unable to keep his hands to himself.

For a man who'd perfected the up-and-out-the-door dash, he felt a surprising lack of panic as Shayna cuddled next to him. Where was the restlessness, the overwhelm-ing need for distance and personal space? Did knowing he was leaving town tomorrow negate his casual, hey that was great, let's do it again sometime attitude?

His feelings were anything but casual. She'd gotten under his skin. Fast. Strange thing was, he wanted to keep her there.

Impossible.

"You're cheating." Shayna's hand traveled dangerously low on his belly as she lifted her head. The strands of hair he'd been toying with slid from his grip. "I can feel your brain waves."

Despite the vigorous lovemaking they'd shared just a few hours ago, his body tightened. He insinuated a leg between hers. "Are you sure it's brain waves you're feeling?"

"Yep. Among other things." Her hand trailed to his rib cage as she knotted her legs around his. "We agreed not to think about tomorrow."

He dipped his head toward the clock. "It *is* tomorrow." And in a few hours, he'd be gone.

"Oh." She rolled on top of him and flipped her hair over

her shoulder, double-checking the glowing red numbers. "Surely it's still yesterday somewhere."

He couldn't see her smile in the darkness, but he certainly heard it. And he agreed one hundred percent. "Hawaii?"

"Aloha," she whispered, her lips grazing the skin above his navel. The silk of her hair tickled as she pushed up and straddled him. He wished the moonlight were brighter so he could see her face. His hands caressed up her stomach, to the heavy weight of her breasts. Words lodged in his throat, words he'd never been tempted to utter before, words he didn't dare consider.

Wishing he could offer her more, hell, everything, he rolled her beneath him and made love to her, for the first time in his life concentrating on emotions rather than finesse. They stroked each other, caressed each other, *loved* each other, then crested and came together.

When their breathing finally leveled out, he held Shayna against his heart, knowing that everything had changed.

A few minutes before sunrise, Shayna felt the loss of Kyle's arms around her body. Lying perfectly still, she listened as he moved around the room, retrieving his clothes and dressing in the dark.

Tears burned behind her closed lids, but she refused to let them fall. She'd invited him here, fully aware of the limitations of what they could offer each other. She wouldn't spoil their one night with a weepy, clingy goodbye.

The mattress sagged near her hip as Kyle leaned down to brush a kiss across her cheek. Without a word, he slipped from the room. Shayna rolled over, buried her face in his leather-scented pillow and let the tears come.

Chapter Thirteen

Chester returned from the deer camp early and agreed to move their appointment up. As she headed into town Thursday afternoon, Shayna rolled her windows down, enjoying the sunshine and crisp, clean air. The return of seasonal weather felt even better after the recent glimpse into winter's bleariness.

Or perhaps the world sparkled brighter because she'd finally made peace with her past. She owed Kyle a huge debt for helping her put old hurts and resentments into perspective. He'd badgered at her and debated with her until she'd had no choice but to reopen old wounds and find ways to heal them for good.

A large chunk of her heart had flown back to L.A. with him Tuesday. But these past few days had given her time to sort through all the facts, all the advice and all the emotions of the past couple of weeks.

Late last night, all the answers she'd been seeking finally became clear. She knew now what she needed to do. She also knew exactly what she was and wasn't willing to do. Her decision was a calculated risk, but it was also the right thing for her.

After scoring a parking spot in the town square, she made her way to the People's Bank building. The four-story building housed most of the professional offices in Holcombe County.

Nelda Parker, Chester's secretary, was seventy if she was a day, but the woman still dressed to impress. Not wanting to stick out like a sore thumb, Shayna had opted for one of her nicest dresses, but she still felt a bit frumpy in comparison to Nelda's navy-and-pink power suit.

"Good morning, Nelda. You look gorgeous as usual."

"Why thank you, dear. You look pretty spiffy yourself."

Shayna ran a smoothing hand over the hip of her brown-and-gold wrap dress. "Thank you."

Nelda stood, revealing a trendy pair of pink Crocs. "Chester said to show you right in, so follow me."

Nelda ushered her into Chester's large, masculine office. Once they'd dealt with the social niceties—everyone was in good health, the weather was wonderful and no one cared for coffee—Shayna got straight to the point.

"Chester, are you aware that James Miller wasn't my natural father?"

"Yes dear, I am." Her surprise must have registered, because he quickly elaborated. "Your Papa Joe and I used to play cards together. When James showed up with you in tow, I asked Joe how come he'd never mentioned becoming a grandfather. He told me then about James adopting you in Boston."

She wanted to let the explanation go at that but knew

Chester's advice wouldn't be worth much if he didn't have all the facts.

"Actually, Daddy never officially adopted me. The courts granted him temporary custody just before Papa Joe got sick, and Daddy and I just never went back."

"Are you worried about the validity of your inheritance, after all these years? Legal paperwork wouldn't have changed y'alls relationship, dear. You were the light of James's life."

"I know that, but—" she filled him in on all the repeated calls to Boston CPS, her missing case files and the forged birth certificate.

"You and I both know that parents often abandon their children without releasing parental rights and those kids are never officially adopted. After all these years, and with no victim to atone to, I can't imagine any judge in this country would be willing to hear a case against your daddy for forgery or fraud. Now, tell me what's really got you this riled up."

Not knowing exactly where to begin, she handed Chester a copy of the dreaded agreement. He adjusted his readers, turned on his desk lamp and started reading. By now, Shayna had read the darn thing so many times she practically had it memorized.

On page four, Chester "uh-huhed," and Shayna charged to her feet, unable to sit still as doubts about her decision raced full tilt around her head. Finally, he finished the last page and looked up.

"Those Hollywood types sure do come up with some wild notions, don't they." Chester's total lack of concern allowed Shayna to release the last of her doubts. Everything was going to work out. Not necessarily smooth and easy, but she didn't mind a few bumps in the road.

"Yes, sir. They sure do, but I've got a few wild notions of my own now."

"I figured you would. Let's hear 'em."

"What's legalese for thanks, but no thanks?"

Travis and Lindy had urged forgiveness. Kyle had made a case for closure and moving on. She'd been fighting to keep her present safe from the past. Daddy had always insisted she follow the right path, no matter how bumpy the road. All the arguments had merit. They all had faults.

In the end, she'd found her solution somewhere in the middle.

Friday morning, Kyle pushed back his leather chair and paced his professionally decorated office, unable to concentrate on the case he'd been reviewing. He wedged a finger inside the neck of his perfectly tailored shirt, struggling against the urge to rip off his tie and unbutton his collar. The world and the clothes that had fit him so well just a week ago no longer felt comfortable.

As they'd done constantly since his return, his thoughts returned to Land's Cross and Shayna. He couldn't believe he'd left her without a word, but the words he'd been tempted to say were too dangerous. Too much stood between them to pretend they had a future. Even saying he'd call would have been wrong, because if he did, the conversation could only revolve around the case.

He expected her father, his biggest client, any minute now. Roscoe had been grudgingly patient with the delay in this case, but Kyle predicted Walker wouldn't be so understanding. His client's deadline was quickly approaching, and like any powerful man, Walker hadn't gotten where he was by adhering to other people's timetables.

A racket in the hall preceeded Amanda's rushed entry, Roscoe and Walker hot on her heels. "Mr. Thomas and Dr. Walker are here to see you, Mr. Anderson."

   As Kyle pushed aside his personal concerns, the two men nearly bowled his secretary over in their rush to enter his office. Amanda, ever the professional, kept her expression serene and offered everyone coffee or water. They all refused.

   She crossed to his desk and handed him an unlabeled folder. "This just came in for you, Mr. Anderson."

   "Thank you, Amanda." Kyle made sure she understood he meant for far more than delivering a fax. She nodded her understanding, sent a meaningful glance at the papers she'd just delivered and then left.

   Curious, Kyle took a quick peek and had to school his features not to reveal his surprise. It was a fax from Chester Warfield. He quickly scanned the short cover letter. Damn it. Shayna had turned down Walker's offer. No counteroffer, no compromise, just a flat no.

   Disappointment and confusion warred for dominance within him, but he tamped them both down. He needed to thoroughly review this paperwork before discussing it with his client, the very client that even now was staring daggers into Kyle's chest.

   Since said client obviously wasn't in a patient mood, Kyle decided to shelve this matter until their next meeting. Putting on his game face, he tucked the papers back inside the folder and turned to welcome the two men.

   The resemblance between Shayna and her biological father was eerie, especially the eyes. Walker's were the same rich color and almond shape as Shayna's; yet at first glance, they seemed lifeless, heartless. Then Walker blinked, and when his eyes reopened, they appeared warm, friendly. It made the resemblance even more striking.

   "So, Anderson, how much longer until you have this little problem wrapped up?"

   Hearing Shayna referred to as a "little problem" lit

Kyle's temper. Taking a deep breath, he moved back into the power position behind his desk and reminded himself that this man's case was the key to his dreams. Soon, he would no longer be forced to work for scumbags like Dr. Steven Walker.

If he could talk some sense into Shayna before Walker got wind of what she'd done.

He dropped the folder onto his desk and waved Walker and Roscoe into the chairs facing him. "Gentlemen, have a seat." He waited until they had complied before continuing. "As I told you yesterday, Ms. Miller has an appointment with her attorney this afternoon." Or at least that was the last he'd heard. Obviously, he was working off old information. "We can't move forward until we hear from them."

"I don't like the fact that you wimped out and gave that silly girl time to contact an attorney. Now this is going to cost me more time and more money."

"The time was necessary, and in the long run it will save you time, money *and* trouble." Kyle weighed his words carefully. He wouldn't lie to his client. That was a rule he couldn't break, not even for Shayna. "If I had coerced her into an agreement without giving her time to seek counsel, she might have sued you later, dragging this whole matter through the press. Isn't avoiding bad press the crux of the job you've hired me to do?"

The words came out smooth, but Kyle's boss, who seemed to recognize the signs of a fraying temper, stepped in, trying to further defuse the situation. "Steven, we've already discussed this. You don't want to come across as some hard-hearted bastard who frightened a young, naive girl into doing something she later regretted. By allowing her time to meet with her attorney, she won't be able to insinuate later that you forced her hand."

"No matter. I've discovered a way to turn this delay to my advantage." Walker reached into the breast pocket of his suit coat and pulled out a sheet of folded paper. "Got an interesting e-mail earlier this morning, with a link to the *Land's Cross Gazette*."

The instant Kyle heard the paper's name, panic tried to take hold, but reason quickly won out. If the man had seen the picture of Kyle dressed as Santa—with Shayna snuggled in his lap—this conversation would not even be taking place. He'd have been fired days ago.

Walker handed the press release to Roscoe. "Seems my long-lost daughter has inherited my interest in giving back. My publicist thinks it would be a great idea if I make a surprise appearance at that little festival of hers, pledge a donation and bond over our mutual love of helping the less fortunate. It would make dynamite footage for the debut show."

Thomas tossed the paper onto Kyle's desk, the gleam in his eyes just as devious as Walker's. Kyle didn't even glance at the page. Tension bunched up painfully in Kyle's shoulders. Surely Thomas would recognize this idea for the train wreck it was.

"I don't know much about television, but it sounds pretty compelling," Thomas answered, doing a damn fine impersonation of a brownnosing yes man.

"Are you out of your mind?" Kyle emphasized his disbelief by banging his fist on the printout lying on his desk. "You can't blindside her like that. You promised her a reasonable period to review the documents with her lawyer, and if you force the issue prematurely, she's likely to balk and refuse to cooperate." Which, technically, she was already trying to do, but since he'd hadn't completely reviewed the document and wasn't ready to discuss it with anyone, he justified keeping his comments hypothetical.

"*I* didn't promise that little bitch anything, Anderson. She probably batted her eyes at you and drawled that sweet southern accent and you couldn't give in fast enough. I'm just lucky you didn't change the terms of the agreement without my approval."

That was taking things too far. Hinting that Kyle had been swayed by Shayna was one thing—hell, it was exactly what had happened. But insinuating that he'd obliterate all ethical standards? That was more than Kyle was willing to take from this arrogant blowhard.

Later that evening as he rushed through the nearly empty Knoxville airport terminal, Kyle finally faced facts. He was in big trouble here. This morning, during his meeting with Walker, he'd skated the ethical lines, his actions and responses balanced precariously on the edge of right versus wrong.

Nothing he'd done or said could be considered, on its own merit, to be a breach of attorney-client privilege. He hadn't given anything other than sound, legal reasons why sending a production crew to film Shayna at the Noel Festival Parade wasn't a smart move. She was guaranteed to freak out, and would, more than likely, halt any and all negotiations, especially if, as Kyle suspected, Patty Hoyt turned out to be Walker's source for Land's Cross social news.

His carefully worded arguments and suggestions hadn't impacted Walker's decision to send a crew. Worse yet, the man was still considering making a cameo appearance. Kyle had done his best to convince his client that his presence would stir up too many questions. Thomas has seconded Kyle's argument, but he wasn't sure Walker had chosen to listen.

Apparently, no one was taking his advice these days.

What the devil was Shayna thinking? Walker would not

react well to her refusal to cooperate. In the back of his mind, he'd expected Shayna's attorney to urge her to ask for more money, maybe pass on the live television program. But declining the entire offer? That just didn't make any sense. Walker was going to persecute her for this.

Unless he could get to her first and make her see reason.

He skidded to a stop in front of the long row of darkened car rental counters. Damn. He'd forgotten to prearrange a vehicle, which meant he'd have to hope there was a cabbie still on duty somewhere in the area willing to drive him out to Land's Cross. Since he'd taken the red-eye out of LAX, it was barely two a.m. here in Tennessee.

Fate must have been working on his side, because when he hit the passenger pickup area he found one cab, its driver sound asleep behind the wheel. After a stiff negotiation— and some serious pleading—he had a ride to Land's Cross.

Kyle spent that dark, quiet hour trying to come up with an excuse for his silent exit Tuesday morning. Any sane man knew better than to walk away from a well-loved woman without a word, especially if you ever wanted her to speak to you again.

Kyle desperately wanted much more than just conversation from Shayna. He flat out wanted her. Which was why he was jacking with his career and jeopardizing his future.

While flying out to Tennessee without his client's approval wasn't enough to get him disbarred, his actions once he got to town very easily could be. It all came down to Walker. If his client pursued actions designed to harm Shayna, Kyle wouldn't be able to stand silently by. And stepping in would be akin to stepping down. The next twelve hours would either make or break his career. So why the hell was he more concerned with Shayna's reaction to his unsanctioned return to Land's Cross than Walker's?

Chapter Fourteen

The setting was soft-focused and beautiful—a gently flowing creek provided the background music and wildflowers carpeted the large open field. Kyle, wearing nothing but her best bathroom towel, laid her out on the bed of sweetly scented flowers. Love shone from his crystal-blue eyes. He smiled at her, that adorable dimple creasing his left cheek.

"Shayna, I have something very important to tell you," he whispered, that deep voice she loved vibrating within her own heart.

Sure he meant to offer the proposal of her dreams, she was all trembling inside. "Yes!" sat on the tip of her tongue, just waiting to be unleashed.

Then Brinks woke her when he sat up, howled for all he was worth and took off downstairs. She slowly opened her eyes, staring up into the darkness. Darn dog. Couldn't he have waited another two minutes?

She started to throw off the covers, but the ringing of the phone stilled her movements. Middle-of-the-night calls were rarely good. She'd left the phone by her bed, hoping Kyle would return the message she'd eventually had no choice but to leave. But would he really call this late? Or had there been an emergency elsewhere?

Deep woofs continued to echo up the stairs. "Hang on," she called to Brinks as she rolled over and snagged the phone. "Hello?"

"Shayna?"

The connection was a bit staticky but there was no mistaking that warm, deep voice she loved so much. "Kyle? What time is it?"

"Too early. I'm sorry, but I was afraid you'd be scared."

Her eyes flicked to the bedside clock—3:27 a.m. "Why?"

"The barking."

The barking? She pushed herself up awkwardly with her elbows and tried to shake the sleep from her brain. "How did you know about that?"

"Brinks is barking at me."

That woke her up. "Where are you?"

"Your front porch."

With a complete lack of self-control that would have embarrassed her had she been fully awake, Shayna slammed the phone shut and jumped out of bed, propelling herself downstairs at breakneck speed. There was no light, but she made her way to the door by habit and yanked it open.

Seeing him on the porch, that familiar black wool coat flapping, snapped some sense back into her. What was she thinking, rushing down here like some heartsick ninny? This man, who'd made fabulous, wonderful, awesome love to her then silently slipped out of her bed, hadn't so much as said boo to her for four days. She couldn't just roll over like Brinks and show him her belly.

At least not until she gave him a moment to apologize.

She backpedaled into the den. "Come in," she directed, grabbing an afghan off the sofa and tossing it around her shoulders.

She turned and found him squatting, petting Brinks, who, as predicted, lay there, paws up, belly exposed. *Way to stay strong, dog,* she thought as she flipped on the lamp. "Kyle?"

He looked up, and the longing in his eyes—like a shipwrecked man who'd just spotted a rescue boat on the horizon—nearly knocked her on her rump. He stood and took several slow steps in her direction, a multitude of thoughts flashing across his expression, none sticking long enough for her to get a handle on. "I shouldn't be here, but I couldn't stay away."

The combination of anguish and sincerity in his voice did her in. Her heart flopped over and gave itself completely, irrevocably, to him.

He came to her and ran the backs of his fingers down her cheek. "I have something very important to tell you, and it couldn't wait until daylight."

The words were so like her dream, Shayna feared she'd pass out from anticipation. "Yes?"

"Monday was the most incredible day of my life, Shayna, starting from the moment you opened the door at the KC Hall until the second I slipped out of your bed. Every hour was perfection, and I'm a complete ass for not telling you sooner."

"You came all this way to tell me that?"

"No. There's more. But that's the most important part, and I needed to make sure you understood that before we tackled anything else."

At this moment there was only one thing Shayna wanted to tackle. Him. She rolled onto the balls of her feet. Giddy lust tickled her toes and raced up through her body.

She really needed to work on camouflaging her expressions, because Kyle seemed to instantly understand her intentions.

"Hang on. That's not what I came here for." His gaze darted to her blanket-covered breasts, giving him away.

"Liar." She laughed, chasing him as he tried to flee. His back hit the door, and this time she had him pinned. Nice.

"Okay, I'd hoped—prayed—we'd eventually end up here but not immediately. Things have changed since Monday. We really need to talk."

"I'm too tired to talk. Let's wait till morning."

"It is morning."

"You're just a regular Big Ben, aren't ya?" She slipped her right hand out from the blanket draped over her shoulders and started toying loose the big buttons on his jacket. She felt rather than heard his sharp intake of breath.

Embracing the full power of her feminine strength, she dropped the afghan, knowing how little her nightgown concealed. His eyes closed. His Adam's apple jumped. She pushed open his overcoat and stepped up, pressing her body against the length of his. Under the thin fabric of her gown, the hard ridge of his arousal pulsed.

Empowered by his response, she tortured them both by shimmying her hips. His erection swelled further. Kyle let his head fall back. She took immediate advantage, nibbling down the exposed length of his throat.

He groaned. "You're making it impossible for me to do the right thing."

"This feels awfully right to me."

"Yeah, it's great, but…" His wide-palmed hands

cupped her cheeks, his thumbs strumming her lips as he tilted her face. Desire flushed his skin and darkened his eyes. Worry bracketed his tightly drawn lips. "I don't want to screw this up."

She pancaked her hands over his. "I know ignoring the future and the differences between us isn't practical, but will a couple of hours really change whatever it is you're so anxious to discuss?"

"No."

"Would it help appease your conscience if I told you I'd been dreaming of making love to you when Brinks woke me?"

She'd begun to lose hope of ever convincing him, so when Kyle's mouth swooped down and stopped her litany of good reasons for making love, it took her a few seconds to catch up.

Goodness, she loved the way this man kissed. It felt as if he wanted to touch all four corners of her soul in one deep breath.

"Tomorrow, we talk." His intensity warmed her every bit as much as the sensual feel of him between her legs.

"Yes, sir." She crawled up his chest, leaving him no choice but to pick her up and carry her upstairs. She worked his buttons loose and nibbled his skin as he made his way through the darkened house.

"Shayna," he growled into her mussed hair. "You're killing me."

Bent at the waist, Shayna tied a towel turban-style around her long, wet hair and stood up, causing the towel wrapped around her breasts to slip. She caught Kyle's stare in the bathroom mirror, his thoughts clearly visible.

"Oh, no, you don't." She wagged a finger at his nearly

naked reflection and cinched up the slipping terry cloth. "Thanks to your remarkable shower skills, I'm already running late."

"Are you complaining?"

"Goodness, no. I've never had such a thorough scrubbing." Warm heat stained her cheeks at the memory of all the places Kyle had kissed and cleaned. "But if you touch me again, I'll never make it to the parade on time."

"So I can look as long as I don't touch?" He settled on the lip of her claw-footed tub, the towel he wore opening to expose a delicious amount of inner thigh.

"I don't think that'll work, either. You're a distraction, Kyle, no matter where you are or what you're doing."

"At least this way, one of us is happy."

"Oh, I didn't say I wasn't happy. Just wonderfully distracted, which I can't afford to be this morning. Please, take pity on me, for the children's sake."

"How about this? I'll go put on some clothes and promise to keep my hands to myself, but I have to stay close. We still have things to discuss."

"Okay, but you have to quit looking at me like that."

"Like what?"

"Like you're picturing me naked."

"But I am." His grin turned wicked. "You've got the most beautiful body, sweetheart." He stood up and crossed the narrow bathroom in a single stride.

"Kyyyyllllle." She drew out his name, desire flaming through her body again. Goodness. This man had turned her into an insatiable wanton. She prayed it would never end, but at the moment, she needed to find a pause button. "Please behave."

"Yes, ma'am. But first…" His lips captured hers in a promise of delights yet to come. Gentle and unhurried, it was the kind of kiss they ran the credits over at the end of a romantic movie.

He released her lips and gave her bare shoulder a teasing nip. "Better cover up fast before I break my promise." He returned to the bedroom, leaving her trembling and hanging on to the bathroom counter for dear life.

Her old green robe hung on the bathroom hook, but Shayna felt the need for more protection. She pulled on a clean pair of jeans and a golden sweater then tackled drying her hair. It would need to be set on rollers before she could twist it into Ms. Noel's fancy updo.

A steamy cup of coffee magically appeared just as she turned off the hair dryer. She took a grateful sip before scanning the small space and finding Kyle, once again perched on the tub. He wore a pair of jeans and a snug white T-shirt under an open flannel shirt whose blue and black pattern really set off his stunning eyes. His feet were bare, which she found uncommonly sexy.

This was getting dangerously close to her idea of domestic bliss.

Concentrate, she ordered herself as she dug out her hot rollers. *Remember the kids.*

"I received the letter from Chester's office yesterday," he said.

Fabulous. He couldn't have picked a less sexy topic. "I tried to call you and tell you about it, but I kept catching your voice mail. I didn't want to tell you such great news in a message."

"Great news? Baby, this isn't great. It's a disaster, and it certainly isn't in your best interest. I can't allow you to submit that letter to Walker. He's not going to respond well."

"I don't care how he responds, although it seems to me the bigger fuss he tries to make for me, the more attention he's going to attract to his mistakes. Once he thinks it over, I'm sure he'll realize it's not a very good idea."

"Oh, you'd be surprised by what that man would consider a good idea."

"Listen, I discussed the whole thing with Chester, and he agrees with me that—"

"Chester isn't as competent as you might think. No lawyer in his right mind advises a client to turn down such a huge settlement offer."

Shayna quickly started twirling her hair around the heated rollers. "A lawyer who understands his client's wishes does. I've never wanted his money for myself, and as for the good that money could do for others, I decided I couldn't sacrifice my own soul, my own principles, not even for that."

She clipped a pin against the final roller and pulled out the bag that held her meager makeup supplies.

He reached the end of the room and spun, stalking back to her. His eyes softened as he ran the backs of his fingers over her cheek. "Shayna, he will destroy your happiness if you don't give him what he wants. He's already taken the first step by arranging—"

"Wait!" she interrupted, her hands flying out between them. His words sparked a light bulb in her brain. "You shouldn't be telling me all this. Scumbag or not, he's your *client.* If anyone finds out about this, won't you be in deep trouble?"

"This is just between us, Shayna. No one will know."

"We'll know, and you'll hate yourself. The one thing you aren't, Kyle, is dishonest. If you violate your client's trust—no matter how much the man doesn't deserve it—it'll haunt you forever."

She pushed to her feet and stepped around Kyle, who hadn't moved a muscle. "Don't say anything else." She double-checked the contents of her makeup bag, added her toothbrush and toothpaste, a handful of hair pins and a can of hairspray. "I'm leaving. Right now. You have to finish this discussion with my attorney, who I promise you is a very sharp and loyal man."

She rushed into the bedroom and grabbed the hanging bag that held her costume and her boots. Remembering her blasted pantyhose, she quickly snatched them from her drawer and wedged the hose and the makeup bag in a side pocket.

A quick mental run-through assured her she had all she needed for her transformation into Ms. Noel. With the rollers still twisted into her hair and her costume draped over her arm, she headed downstairs to find her purse and her keys. Kyle followed her down the stairs, trying to resume their conversation.

"It's not a technical violation of attorney-client privilege."

"Technicalities don't change the truth. I can't let you do this."

Her purse sat on the kitchen table, a few feet from where Brinks waited patiently for his breakfast and his morning walk.

"Walker is no longer my primary concern. You—"

Man, she wanted to hear the end of that sentence, but she couldn't let himself dig this hole any deeper. Purse on her shoulder, she leaned in and interrupted him with a kiss.

The heavy costume on her arm and the warm rollers on her head affected her balance and technique, but she still managed to stop his flow of self-incriminating words.

When she pulled back, they were both a bit dazed.

"Oh, and one other thing I've been meaning to tell you."

"I don't know if I can take any more revelations this morning, Shayna."

"This one's easy. The other night, I forgot to tell Santa what I wanted for Christmas, and I was wondering if you could give him a message from me."

The dazed shake of his head was part agitation, part admiration. "What do you want Santa to bring you this year, little girl?"

"You." She laid another hot, quick kiss on him. "All I want is you."

Standing in the People's Bank parking lot decked out in full Ms. Noel regalia, Shayna was still high from the stunned look on Kyle's face. Her wish had definitely taken him by surprise, but judging by the way his lips had clung to hers, she was pretty sure it was a good surprise.

Happy enough to power every Christmas light in town, she surveyed the chaotic scene around her. The parade gods were certainly smiling down on them today. The morning's crisp air had everyone in a Christmas mood. The sun dangled in a cloudless, endless blue sky, adding just enough warmth that the Fighting Lion cheerleaders didn't have to wear sweatpants under their short skirts. Concession stands scented the air with funnel cakes, apple cider and sausage on a stick.

Perfect day for a parade.

A series of horn blasts announced the arrival of the youth center van as it entered the parking lot. The van's door slid open, coughing out a dozen excited, costumed children. Their giggles and shouts carried across the crowd of parade riders and volunteers. Nothing summed up the joy of Christmas like a bunch of happy, hopeful kids.

She spied Danny making his way across the lot, flanked by his two precious daughters, Shelley and Tina, the reigning Junior Miss Noel. Tina would ride next to Shayna on the princess float. Danny, filling in as Santa since Elmer's back was still out, was the parade's grand finale, and as such, would be on the final float. Shelley would watch from the sidelines with Lindy and Travis.

After Shayna, Shelley and Tina had finished complimenting each other's dresses, Danny, wearing the new, longer Santa pants she'd made for him, cleared his throat and nodded to his left. "Did you call out one of the major networks?"

"No. As far as I know, channel five is the only station planning on covering the parade. Why?" She looked over her shoulder, where a three-person television crew stood off to the side, panning shots of the pandemonium. None of them wore channel five's signature bright blue jackets. "Oh. Well, extra publicity can't hurt, right?"

"No, but I'm not real jazzed about the whole state seeing me in this getup."

"Don't worry. Once you get the padding and beard on, no one will recognize you."

"I sure as hell hope so."

"Daddy." Shelley and Tina scolded together.

"Sorry, girls." Danny gave a chagrined smile. "Let's go find Lindy. It's time for all of us to take our places."

The next several minutes were a whirlwind of confusion. Nerves needed to be calmed, dresses needed to be fluffed, float decorations needed to be repaired, and for some reason, all these calamities ended up in her lap.

Once she had the barrage of last-minute details ironed out, she looked again for the production crew. Their presence had niggled around her thoughts, and she'd begun to question their purpose. Their lack of obvious station affiliation bothered her.

Hitching herself up on the princess trailer, she surveyed the crowd. A reporter she recognized interviewed the high school band's tuba section. The crew surrounding her wore distinctive blue jackets.

A gaggle of goose bumps sprang up on her arms as she searched for the second, obviously well-funded crew. Her bad feeling quickly grew to a pit-of-the-stomach dread.

Finally she spotted them, standing on a knoll, high enough to take in all the activity in a single shot. Standing slightly behind the camera operator was a squat fellow she'd never met but recognized instantly.

Steven Walker.

Cold sweat covered Shayna's body. What the hell was he doing here? Was this what Kyle had tried to warn her about? Her hands began to shake so badly she had to grip a waist-high candy cane to keep herself upright.

Why, oh why hadn't she taken the low road and greedily listened to all the secrets Kyle had been anxious to spill?

Because Walker can no longer hurt you.

Just as quickly as the panic had spread a moment ago, peace now settled over her. She had nothing to fear from this man. Still, it might be best not to confront him until Walker also knew about his loss of negotiating power. No sense airing all that dirty laundry prematurely.

Before she got carried away imagining the stunned look on Walker's perennially smug face, Shayna brought her attention back to today's event. Parade time was almost here.

Trucks and tractors fired up, the rattle of diesel engines adding to the roar of excited voices. Recorded Christmas carols blared out over the PA system while the marching band tuned up.

She prepared to jump down and help the little ones line up, but from the corner of her eye she noticed a familiar blond head pushing his way to Walker's side. Even from this distance, the anger and disappointment on Kyle's face was clear.

He was obviously seconds away from telling off his biggest client and sabotaging his career. She couldn't let him do that, not when the misguided man still thought she needed his protection.

She loved him too much to stand aside and watch him throw away a goal he'd worked half a lifetime for. No matter how good his intentions.

As the other parade princesses began climbing aboard the float, Shayna jumped off. She waved at a surprised, fully costumed Danny and started running through the scurrying crowd.

Behind her, Danny shouted her name, but she didn't slow down, didn't look back.

Her focus remained pinned on Kyle and Walker. Judging by the hand gestures and the distance the crew had given the two men, things were not going well.

By the time she reached them, Shayna was completely breathless. She had to stand there pulling in deep draws of air before she could alert them to her arrival.

"I haven't been too impressed with your advice, Anderson, so I made an executive decision." Walker was puffed up and red in the face.

"Surprising her isn't the right way to handle this. You should have at least shown her the courtesy of an advance warning."

"Advance warning?" That shrill voice stole what little breath Shayna had managed to recover. Dressed in white leather pants and an indecently tight red sweater, Patty stepped from behind a long, solid-paneled white van. "Isn't that what you were giving my baby girl when you slipped inside her cabin this morning? Or maybe you were too busy slipping her something else?"

Her mother's crude comment drew a loud hiss from Shayna, but Kyle's "What the hell is *she* doing here?" overpowered the sound.

"I'm just here to enjoy the festivities," Patty replied in a frighteningly normal voice. "And to support my beautiful daughter, of course."

"Bull!" Shayna thundered her way into the conversation. She'd had enough of her vindictive birth parents and their nonsense. "You're both here to intimidate me into reconsidering my refusal."

"What refusal?" Walker shoved Patty aside, turning confused eyes to Kyle. "She responded and you didn't tell me?"

Kyle nodded, but his attention remained focused on her. This morning's intimate warmth was nowhere to be seen. "We received a fax yesterday, but I didn't forward it because Ms. Miller's response was ill-advised and poorly conceived. I was hoping to convince her to reissue the offer with a more acceptable set of demands."

Shayna wasn't sure which hurt more. The fact that the love of her life had just essentially called her an idiot or the ease with which he slipped back into power attorney mode.

Ms. Miller, indeed.

Even though she knew the two of them didn't have a future together, it still stung to be so soundly reminded.

Knowing a clean break would be best for them both, Shayna called up every ounce of poise and self-control in her body. Back straight and head held high, she turned her back on Kyle and addressed her worthless, conniving parents.

"If you two want to continue to torture each other over a relationship that soured twenty-five years ago, then go right ahead, but I refuse to let either of you drag me into this mess ever again. I won't take sides, and I won't absolve either of you for the horrible way you treated me. From here on out, I never want to hear from either of you again."

Their shocked, blanched expressions were priceless. She wished she had a camera, but then, she imagined the little red light on the huge television camera meant Walker's own people were capturing this moment much better than her little digital ever could.

Unable to bring herself to look in Kyle's direction, Shayna started to head back to her float—somehow, she had to rise to her role as parade hostess—but Kyle's fingers captured her wrist.

"Shayna?"

In that moment, staring into the vivid eyes she loved so much, her heart actually felt broken. How could she have forgotten that she was nothing more than a case, the means of getting that promotion?

Drawing the shards of her pride up from where it had crashed around her ankles, Shayna stiffened her spine and forced the tears from her voice. "Mr. Anderson, my apologies for getting carried away earlier today. As you can see—" she swooped her hands dramatically over her costume "—I'm a Christmas fanatic. Now, if you'll excuse me, I don't want to hold up the parade."

A shadow fell over Kyle's face. Shayna looked over her shoulder, but the entire parade crowd was blocked by a large red wall. "Shayna, what's going on here? Are you okay?"

She offered Danny a wobbly smile. "Yeah. Looks like you were right about the extra camera crew. I've explained that they're not wanted here. Hopefully, they'll clear out soon."

"What about him?" He indicated Kyle with a head nod.

Swallowing her heartbreak, she strove for a light tone.

"I do believe Mr. Anderson's business here is finished. I'm
sure he'll be leaving soon, as well." Quickly, please.

"I'm not going anywhere."

"Fine. I hope you enjoy the parade." Afraid the tears
would start flowing any second, she headed back to her
post. She didn't hear the actual words spoken, but she
knew that behind her, Danny and Kyle had a short standoff.
She held her breath, expecting—praying—Kyle would
stop her at any second.

When she reached the princess float unscathed, she knew
Kyle wouldn't be coming after her. Not today. Not ever.

It took a lot of fast talking for Kyle to reassure Danny
that he had no intention of further upsetting Shayna. At
least not until after the parade. The big man made an effective bodyguard, but the spark in his eyes and the smirk
on his face gave him away. Danny Robertson was no more
a physical threat than Brinks.

Brinks was okay, but Danny had to go. From here on out,
Kyle planned to be the man covering Shayna's back. And
her front, but he had to take it one step at a time for now.

As Danny sprinted back to his Santa float, Kyle
followed the van's progress through the thick crowds and
blocked roads. His pedestrian status gave him a huge advantage today. Catching up with his fleeing client would
be no problem.

Walking westward, he quickly caught up with the white
production van at a stoplight. He motioned the driver into
an adjacent parking lot and waited for Walker to disembark.

There were some critical issues he needed to straighten
out with his client. Before he quit.

This case had shone a bright light on the holes in his
childhood dream. Happiness was about a hell of a lot more

than money, power and prestige. It was about love and laughter and making a positive impact.

For years, his life had centered around making partner, and he'd come damn close to making that goal a reality. Too damn close. He'd been one deal away from sealing his fate, from spending the rest of his worthless life helping selfish people avoid answering for their mistakes, from never experiencing any joy in his life.

Thank God he'd finally wised up and realized there was something he wanted even more than all that crap.

Shayna.

She was the future he'd been searching for. The place didn't matter. The job didn't matter. Shayna was all he needed.

He prayed he wasn't too late to convince her they belonged together. Surely she could see it. They made a good team, and now they had the same goals.

And he loved her.

It was as simple and as complicated as that.

Chapter Fifteen

For the umpteenth time, Shayna reminded herself to think of the kids as she clutched her damp palms together and entered the Moonlight and Mistletoe Ball. Solo.

Stop that. Celebrate now, fall apart later.

Plastering her parade smile back on her face, she paused inside the gym's double doors. Her breath caught in her throat.

Beautiful.

A rotating disco ball hung from the center of the room, where the ceiling soared to twenty feet. Colored lights danced all through the huge room. Boughs of mistletoe hung from every imaginable spot and fully decorated Christmas trees were scattered throughout.

Overhead, thousands of plastic stars twinkled. It was like standing under a winter night's sky without dealing with the cold weather.

The festival spirit began to take root as she mingled.

Everyone she spoke with said it was the best festival ever. Of course, they said that every year, but still, having played such a public role this year, Shayna couldn't help but bask in all the compliments. Under any other circumstances, she'd feel like the belle of the ball.

She certainly looked the part. Like most women in town, she'd splurged on a new outfit for tonight's party. The sequined red gown fit like a dream. The thigh-high slit running up her right side drew the attention of every man in the room.

But the only man whose attention she was interested in was probably already back in sunny California. Small towns being what they were, Kyle's absence made him a hot topic, and it seemed as if everyone had asked about him at least twice already.

If she weren't such a big chicken, she'd have told them he wasn't coming because she'd run him off. Instead, she hemmed and hawed, telling them she wasn't sure about his plans. The truth, yes—but not exactly an honest answer.

She lowered her guard for a few minutes when Lindy and Travis showed up with Danny and his family. Danny, who looked stellar in a black pin-striped suit and gold vest, immediately asked her to dance.

"Still okay?" When it came to looking out for those he cared for, the man was like a dog with a bone, and she loved him for it.

"A little shell-shocked, but hanging in there."

"Heard from Kyle?"

"Nope." Her feet stumbled. "He's gone."

Danny covered her misstep flawlessly. "You sure about that? He told me he had stuff to take care of, then he would catch up with you after the parade."

His words perked up her hopelessly devoted heart, but

she refused to drop her guard completely. "Guess he meant Monday, during business hours."

"It didn't sound to me like he had business on the brain."

"What else could it be? Wrapping up this case is crucial to his career."

"I saw the way he looked at you, sweetie. That man was not thinking about his career."

"Those steamy looks were just chemistry."

"If memory serves, sex—no matter how good—doesn't make a man go all moony. My money says he's as much in love with you as you are with him."

This time she didn't stumble. She came to a dead stop, ignoring all the other dancers. "It's that obvious?"

"Yep." Danny grinned, pulling her back into the music's flow. "You both practically vibrate when the other gets close."

"If that's true, then where is he?"

The music ended. Shayna stepped slowly out of Danny's arms and joined the applause for the band.

"Over there," Danny whispered near her ear, pointing toward the side entrance. Her stomach dropped to her knees. Even across the vast gym, seeing Kyle again, dressed in a dark suit and red-and-gold tie, nearly knocked her socks off.

Every muscle in her body quivered with the desire to run to him and throw her arms around his neck, but her injured pride refused to cooperate. Still, as she worked the room, her progress did take her slowly but surely in his direction.

Finally they stood face-to-face, off to the edge of the crowd. "You look amazing," he said.

"Yes, well, as head volunteer, it's expected."

"Shayna, we have important things that need to be said. In private. Things I tried to tell you last night, before you distracted me."

"Distracted you? Is that what you call it? Funny, I had a whole different phrase for it."

"Please. Give me five minutes, so I can explain what happened earlier."

The band wound down their final song of the set, and the sudden quiet made the room seem larger, louder somehow.

"This is not a good time." She felt as jumpy as the last cricket in the bait bucket. Which made this whole mess worse since she was scheduled to speak during the intermission.

Mayor Evans took the stage, leaving her only a few minutes to compose her nerves. Kyle tried again. "Shayna—" A burst of applause interrupted his plea, and warned her she'd been introduced.

Gritting her teeth beneath a wide grin, she forced herself to calmly ascend the steps. "Thank you, Mayor Evans, and thank you, Holcombe County. Without you, none of this would be possible."

She smiled wider and applauded the crowd, who applauded right back. As she looked out into the sea of mostly familiar faces, snippets of her memorized speech flashed inside her brain, along with memories of this year's festival, images of Kyle, as Santa and as himself. The words she'd planned lodged in her throat as she watched him approach the front of the stage.

He stopped directly in front of her. The festive lighting's ambient glow played tricks with her vision, making her think for a moment she saw love burning in Kyle's eyes.

Surely that was just wishful thinking, right?

Unconcerned about the five hundred or so people milling around them, he announced, "I have something very important I need to tell you, Shayna."

She cupped her hand over the microphone—not that she needed to bother. The huge room was suddenly as quiet as church on Monday. "I'm kind of in the middle of something here," she whispered through clenched teeth. "Can't this wait?"

"No." Forgoing the risers, he stepped up on center stage, right next to her. "Every time I try to tell you something important, you cut me off. I'm tired of waiting."

Flustered, she blinked out at the wide-eyed crowd. It seemed as if everyone she knew was out there, holding their breaths, dying to hear what Kyle had to say.

This was a little too small-town-in-your-business even for her. "Not here, Kyle. Give me five min—"

"Right here, right now." He took her shoulders and turned her away from the crowd, leaving her no choice but to meet his gaze. Vivid, honest emotions swam in his bright blue eyes.

Hope, joy and longing sprang to life in her heart, and this time she did nothing to hold them back. "I was afraid you'd gone back to California."

His hand cupped her jaw, his thumbs caressing her bottom lip. She could feel the speed of his pulse. "I told you I wasn't going anywhere."

A tug on her skirt startled her. One look at the unspoken words in Kyle's eyes and she'd forgotten all about the crowd surrounding them. Following the pressure on her hem, she looked down, where Tommy Hunter stood next to her, pointing up.

"Mistletoe, Miz Shayna. You know what that means."

The fire in her face could have melted snow. Shayna tried for the coward's way out, reaching for Tommy's thin shoulders. "No! Not me. Kiss Mr. Kyle." He jumped off the stage and scurried back into the crowd.

Mortified, she snuck a peek at the crowd, praying no one had heard the child's command. No such luck. Everyone seemed to be smiling and glancing between the sprig of greenery hanging from the ceiling and the couple on the stage.

"Come on, Anderson!" Someone in the crowd—someone who sounded an awful lot like Danny Robertson—shouted. "Kiss her."

The room swelled with chants of, "Kiss, kiss, kiss."

Not certain her heart would ever beat steadily again, Shayna faced Kyle.

"May I?" he asked.

"Yes."

His lips seized hers, not in the chaste peck the crowd had probably expected but in a gentle, lingering caress that turned her muscles to mush.

Behind them, the band began to tune up, signaling the imminent return of dancing and celebrating. She knew this public display had gone way beyond the bounds of mere affection, but she felt helpless to bring the kiss to an end.

Finally the pressure of Kyle's lips against hers began to lessen. His fingers trembled as he released her face and stepped back. The band's lead singer slapped Kyle's back. "Awesome kiss, dude. Now, how 'bout clearing the stage?"

"You bet. How 'bout playing something slow?"

Shayna was still waiting for the feeling to return to her toes when Kyle linked their fingers and drew her off the stage and onto the dance floor. The soft strains of "The Lady in Red" filled the ballroom as Kyle folded her into his arms and began to sway.

"I couldn't leave. There's still way too much unfinished business between us," he said softly.

Unsure how to respond, she tucked her head under his chin and just concentrated on moving her feet.

Tears burned her eyes. Business? Did that mean the emotions she'd seen on his face were all an illusion? Had she let Danny's words and her hopeful heart convince her that the impossible had happened, that Kyle had chosen her over his career?

The last note hanging in the air, Kyle's lips brushed across her ear. "Is there somewhere we can talk?"

Still unable to find her voice, she pointed toward a back set of double doors that led outside to a balcony overlooking the courtyard. Kyle nodded in agreement, and they wove their way across the dance floor in silence. Shayna walked to the far side of the deserted balcony and leaned over the railing. The tears brimming in her eyes cast halos around the Christmas lights hung all around downtown.

Sudden warmth enveloped her as Kyle draped his jacket over her shoulders. The material carried the heat and smell of him. Desperate to appear in control, she smiled her thanks. "So, what's this unfinished business that couldn't wait?"

"I quit my job."

"You did?" Stunned, she spun and faced him. "But you worked so hard to make partner. I thought it was your dream job."

"I did, too, until I realized I had a new dream."

All the moisture in her mouth dried up. She had to swallow twice before she could speak. "What is it?"

"I set those goals when I was fifteen. I had just narrowly escaped arrest, and that caused me to take stock of my life. As you'd guessed, at that point the only men I'd ever met who qualified as role models were the attorneys who work with children's services. My twisted teenage brain put two and two together and came up with a long list of shallow traits that made a man worthy." His lips quirked, as if he found the boy he used to be amusing.

"But now, fifteen years later, I realize that what really makes a man worthy isn't what he gets out of the world but what he gives back, not what he possesses but what he treasures. You, Shayna, are what I treasure."

The hope she'd harbored in her heart bloomed, engulfed her, stole her power of speech. She clutched her hands around his jacket, still draped around her shoulders, and waited.

His hands slipped around her and pulled her to his chest. "I don't think I've ever seen you speechless."

"Guess there's a first time for everything," she said hesitantly.

"Like the first time I tell you I love you?"

Robbed of her speech again, she could only nod.

He bent his knees and brought their eyes level. "I love you, Shayna Miller." His lips neared hers but veered off at the last second, skimming over her cheek. "No response?" he asked before sucking her earlobe between his lips, sending a sensual shock wave straight to her core and restoring all her powers.

She unwedged her hands from between their chests and wrapped her arms around his neck. "I love you, too. So much."

She laid her cheek against his heart and squeezed. His arms responded, holding her tighter. She felt his lips graze her forehead.

"Please say you'll marry me."

"I'll marry you," she promised. "Right here, right now, if you want."

"I need time to buy a ring."

"It's not about the possessions. It's about the treasures, and I'm going to treasure this moment forever."

"And I'm going to treasure *you* forever."

Smiling so hard her cheeks hurt, she lifted her head and indicated the garland-wrapped awning with a lift of her eyes. "I think you should kiss me. There's at least fifty bunches of mistletoe hanging over our heads."

"Whose idea was that?"

"Well, I *did* help decorate."

"So you set me up?"

"Maybe. Maybe not. But either way, I figure I've got fifty kisses coming my way."

"How about fifty years of kisses?"

"Um, I like the sound of that."

Kyle's jacket slipped to the ground as Shayna drew his mouth down to hers. Moonlight and mistletoe formed a halo around them, and Shayna knew the memory of this moment would be forever imprinted in her mind and her heart.

She'd definitely gotten her Christmas wish.

* * * * *

Celebrate 60 years of pure reading pleasure with Harlequin®!
Just in time for the holidays,
Silhouette Special Edition® is proud to present
New York Times *bestselling author*
Kathleen Eagle's
ONE COWBOY, ONE CHRISTMAS

Rodeo rider Zach Beaudry was a travelin' man—until he broke down in middle-of-nowhere South Dakota during a deep freeze. That's when an angel came to his rescue....

"**D**on't die on me. Come on, Zel. You know how much I love you, girl. You're all I've got. Don't do this to me here. Not *now*."

But Zelda had quit on him, and Zach Beaudry had no one to blame but himself. He'd taken his sweet time hitting the road, and then miscalculated a shortcut. For all he knew he was a hundred miles from gas. But even if they were sitting next to a pump, the ten dollars he had in his pocket wouldn't get him out of South Dakota, which was not where he wanted to be right now. Not even his beloved pickup truck, Zelda, could get him much of anywhere on fumes. He was sitting out in the cold in the middle of nowhere. And getting colder.

He shifted the pickup into Neutral and pulled hard on the steering wheel, using the downhill slope to get her off the blacktop and into the roadside grass, where she shuddered to a standstill. He stroked the padded dash. "You'll be safe here."

But Zach would not. It was getting dark, and it was already too damn cold for his cowboy ass. Zach's battered body was a barometer, and he was feeling South Dakota, big-time. He'd have given his right arm to be climbing into a hotel hot tub instead of a brutal blast of north wind. The right was his free arm anyway. Damn thing had lost altitude, touched some part of the bull and caused him a scoreless ride last time out.

It wasn't scoring him a ride this night, either. A carload of teenagers whizzed by, topping off the insult by laying on the horn as they passed him. It was at least twenty minutes before another vehicle came along. He stepped out and waved both arms this time, damn near getting himself killed. Whatever happened to *do unto others?* In places like this, decent people didn't leave each other stranded in the cold.

His face was feeling stiff, and he figured he'd better start walking before his toes went numb. He struck out for a distant yard light, the only sign of human habitation in sight. He couldn't tell how distant, but he knew he'd be hurting by the time he got there, and he was counting on some kindly old man to answering the door. No shame among the lame.

It wasn't like Zach was fresh off the operating table— it had been a few months since his last round of repairs— but he hadn't given himself enough time. He'd lopped a couple of weeks off the near end of the doc's estimated recovery time, rigged up a brace, done some heavy-duty taping and climbed onto another bull. Hung in there for five seconds—four seconds past feeling the pop in his hip and three seconds short of the buzzer.

He could still feel the pain shooting down his leg with

every step. Only this time he had to pick the damn thing up, swing it forward and drop it down again on his own.

Pride be damned, he just hoped *somebody* would be answering the door at the end of the road. The light in the front window was a good sign.

The four steps to the covered porch might as well have been four hundred, and he was looking to climb them with a lead weight chained to his left leg. His eyes were just as screwed up as his hip. Big black spots danced around with tiny red flashers, and he couldn't tell what was real and what wasn't. He stumbled over some shrubbery, steadied himself on the porch railing and peered between vertical slats.

There in the front window stood a spruce tree with a silver star affixed to the top. Zach was pretty sure the red sparks were all in his head, but the white lights twinkling by the hundreds throughout the huge tree, those were real. He wasn't too sure about the woman hanging the shiny balls. Most of her hair was caught up on her head and fastened in a curly clump, but the light captured by the escaped bits crowned her with a golden halo. Her face was a soft shadow, her body a willowy silhouette beneath a long white gown. If this was where the mind ran off to when cold started shutting down the rest of the body, then Zach's final worldly thought was, *This ain't such a bad way to go.*

If she would just turn to the window, he could die looking into the eyes of a Christmas angel.

* * * * *

*Could this woman from Zach's past get the lonesome
cowboy to come in from the cold...for good?
Look for
ONE COWBOY, ONE CHRISTMAS
by Kathleen Eagle.
Available December 2009 from
Silhouette Special Edition®.*

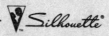

SPECIAL EDITION

**FROM *NEW YORK TIMES* AND *USA TODAY*
BESTSELLING AUTHOR**

KATHLEEN EAGLE

ONE COWBOY,
One Christmas

When bull rider Zach Beaudry appeared
out of thin air on Ann Drexler's ranch,
she thought she was seeing a ghost of
Christmas past. And though Zach had
no memory of their night of passion years
ago, they were about to share a future
he would never forget.

*Available December 2009
wherever books are sold.*

SSE65493

Visit Silhouette Books at www.eHarlequin.com

REQUEST YOUR FREE BOOKS!
2 FREE NOVELS PLUS 2 FREE GIFTS!

SPECIAL EDITION®
Life, Love and Family!

YES! Please send me 2 FREE Silhouette Special Edition® novels and my 2 FREE gifts (gifts are worth about $10). After receiving them, if I don't wish to receive any more books, I can return the shipping statement marked "cancel." If I don't cancel, I will receive 6 brand-new novels every month and be billed just $4.24 per book in the U.S. or $4.99 per book in Canada. That's a savings of at least 15% off the cover price! It's quite a bargain! Shipping and handling is just 50¢ per book.* I understand that accepting the 2 free books and gifts places me under no obligation to buy anything. I can always return a shipment and cancel at any time. Even if I never buy another book from Silhouette, the two free books and gifts are mine to keep forever.

235 SDN EYN4   335 SDN EYPG

Name	(PLEASE PRINT)	
Address		Apt. #
City	State/Prov.	Zip/Postal Code

Signature (if under 18, a parent or guardian must sign)

Mail to the **Silhouette Reader Service:**
IN U.S.A.: P.O. Box 1867, Buffalo, NY 14240-1867
IN CANADA: P.O. Box 609, Fort Erie, Ontario L2A 5X3

Not valid to current subscribers of Silhouette Special Edition books.

Want to try two free books from another line?
Call 1-800-873-8635 or visit www.morefreebooks.com.

* Terms and prices subject to change without notice. Prices do not include applicable taxes. Sales tax applicable in N.Y. Canadian residents will be charged applicable provincial taxes and GST. Offer not valid in Quebec. This offer is limited to one order per household. All orders subject to approval. Credit or debit balances in a customer's account(s) may be offset by any other outstanding balance owed by or to the customer. Please allow 4 to 6 weeks for delivery. Offer available while quantities last.

Your Privacy: Silhouette is committed to protecting your privacy. Our Privacy Policy is available online at www.eHarlequin.com or upon request from the Reader Service. From time to time we make our lists of customers available to reputable third parties who may have a product or service of interest to you. If you would prefer we not share your name and address, please check here. ☐

SSE09R